Clangor in the Bell Tower

Mab Graff

ACCENT BOOKS
Denver, Colorado

MEMBER OF
EVANGELICAL CHRISTIAN
PUBLISHERS ASSOCIATION

ACCENT BOOKS
A Division of Accent-B/P Publications, Inc.
12100 W. Sixth Avenue
P.O. Box 15337
Denver, Colorado 80215

Library of Congress Catalog Card Number: 77-91493

ISBN 0-916406-89-X

1

There was a subtle, downward movement inside the plane, and my heart began to pump so hard I could feel it in my throat.

The voice over the speaker system was relaxed and resonant. "Ladies and gentlemen, this is your captain. We are beginning our descent into Los Angeles and should be landing in approximately fifteen minutes."

The FASTEN SEAT BELTS sign came on and, as I fumbled with the cold buckle, I could feel perspiration breaking out on my forehead and in the palms of my hands. But I wasn't afraid because we were landing. My panic was because I was going to a new job in a huge city, where I didn't know one single person.

My mind whirled with unanswered questions. What would it be like to be a pastor's secretary? What if I didn't like the work—or him? Worse—what if he didn't like me? I undoubtedly would do something stupid the first day.

And then, there was the school. Meeting new people sure wasn't one of my favorite things. My stomach began to feel like a steel ball.

For about the fifth time during the flight, I took the letter out of my purse and read the letterhead:

ARBOLEDA HEIGHTS CHRISTIAN CHURCH
AND SCHOOL
1700 Arroyo Drive, Arboleda Heights, California 92630

The letter had been flawlessly typed:

> Miss Louise Bridges
> 314 Sequoia Avenue
> Portland, Oregon 97222
>
> Dear Miss Bridges:
>   We are glad you feel led to accept the position of church secretary, and this is to confirm your arrival at Los Angeles International Airport on April 1, at 9:30 a.m.

Mr. Gerald Loop, a trusted member of the church, will meet you. He is middle-aged, tall, and has white hair.

I trust you will have no difficulty meeting him.

Sincerely in Christ,

Richard S. Fitzsimmons, Pastor

I put the letter back in my purse and looked out the window. The houses below were beginning to look bigger and, in spite of an overcast, I could see hundreds of turquoise-colored spots shimmering in the thin sunlight. Every fifth house seemed to have a pool—and I had never seen so many cars!

My shoulder blades burned with tension as the tires squawked on the runway. The big plane whined its way slowly into docking position and most of the passengers stood up.

What if I couldn't find Mr. Gerald Loop, I worried, as I followed a man up the tunneled ramp to the waiting room.

Well then, stupid, I spoke to myself, you go to the phone and call the church. But almost immediately I saw the tall, distinguished-looking Mr. Loop. His hair was brilliantly white and very wavy, and his bushy eyebrows were also white. His shoe-button eyes gleamed with a friendly light.

"Miss Bridges?" He stepped around the rope and smiled.

"Yes." I made myself smile and my shoulders relaxed a little. He had a tiny, white toothbrush mustache and, in contrast, his square teeth looked slightly yellow.

"How did you know me?" I asked as he led me toward the escalator.

"You were the first young lady to come off the plane alone." He smiled down at me. "My plan was to ask each single lady until I found you."

I laughed and decided he was pretty smart. I also decided I liked Mr. Loop. He was slender and, although his hair made him seem old, his face was unlined and youthful.

"I guess the first thing we'd better do is get your luggage," he said as we left the escalator. We walked down an interminable corridor.

As we waited for my two suitcases, he made small talk. "I understand Pastor Fitzsimmons is delighted to have a secretary again."

"I hope I can please him," I murmured, although I was reasonably sure I could do the work in a church office. I had graduated from one of the best business schools in Portland.

In periodic bouts of silence, we watched hundreds of pieces of luggage spin slowly before us.

"Have you ever worked before, Miss Bridges?"

"Oh, yes. I quit a job with a law firm to come down here."

"Is that right?" Mr. Loop seemed impressed. "I hope you won't be sorry." I looked at him, but his eyes were on the luggage.

"I hope not, too!" I said, "But I don't think I will. My job with the attorneys was very dull. All I ever did was type wills or mortgage papers." He made a sympathetic face.

"Didn't you ever get to go to trials or anything exciting?"

"No!" I shook my head and grinned. "I was the youngest stenographer, so if there were any special assignments, the men took the older stenos. The only thing I ever got to do that was exciting was to take notes at an inquest where a young girl had been killed on a ski lift."

"You mean verbatim notes?"

"Yes."

"You must be pretty good."

I blushed. "Well, I got it all and got it transcribed. But that was several months ago—and I haven't used my shorthand since." I thought about the quiet, dull law office and shuddered. I was glad I wasn't there this morning.

"How did you happen to know about the job at our church, Miss Bridges?"

"Mr. Loop, would you call me Louise? It seems so strange to be called Miss Bridges."

"All right, then. Louise it is! And you can call me Gerald." I glanced at him and knew I would never be able to call him anything but Mr. Loop.

"So—how did you come to apply for the job?" he asked again.

"Do you know Beverly Wrightwood!"

"Indeed I do." He rubbed his mustache with his fingertips. "Our elementary school would fall on its face without her. She's supposed to be the school secretary, but she runs the place." He shook his head in wonder.

"Well, my Aunt Bertha and Mrs. Wrightwood went to school together, and they have kept their friendship all these years."

"Isn't that remarkable!"

I nodded. "She wrote to my aunt a few weeks ago and happened to mention that Reverend Fitzsimmons was looking for a secretary. So, Aunt Bertha and I talked it over. I've been living with her the last year, and she knew how boring my job was, and also that I'd been wanting to move away from Portland. So, she called Mrs. Wrightwood and told her about me. Then Mrs. Wrightwood told Reverend Fitzsimmons, and he was interested, so I sent him my qualifications." I shrugged and smiled up at him. "So—he hired me."

Mr. Loop stared at me with his brown, button eyes and I could feel my cheeks begin to redden. Why did we have to keep talking? I felt as though I was on trial. I looked away and wished my suitcases would come.

"Then—you've never met the pastor?" Something in his tone made me turn quickly.

"No, I never have." I bit the edge of my lip as I studied his face. Was there something strange about the pastor? But Mr. Loop's face was inscrutable.

"What is he like?" I asked.

Mr. Loop's eyes flicked up and down slowly as he watched suitcases go by. He put his hands in his pockets and pursed his lips.

"He's a fine preacher," he said thoughtfully. "All of us have grown spiritually under his preaching."

And yet, his tone seemed to imply—and yet what? I wondered. Or was I only imagining a reserve in Mr. Loop, a certain unspoken criticism?

Before I could worry about it, I saw one of my old, brown suitcases gliding toward us. "There's one!" I cried and started to reach out, but Mr. Loop deftly grabbed it.

"You're right," he smiled, "and I'll bet that's the other one."

"It is!" I was relieved. It had been hard for me to make small talk and try to be at ease with this stranger, even though

6

he had been exceptionally kind.

As we left the building, I was aware of an overwhelming, oily smell which made my eyes begin to burn. I dug around in my purse for a tissue.

"I see our smog has gotten to you," he sympathized, as I blew my nose. "It's extra heavy today. Actually, I don't know why any of us live here."

He started across the street and I followed, almost running. Even with my five foot-seven inch, long-legged frame, it was hard to keep up.

"In some ways, though," he said over his shoulder, "Los Angeles is the most marvelous place in the world."

He led the way through a maze of parked cars, and I was surprised when he stopped at a small, blue Porsche. He popped open the trunk, deposited my suitcases, and quickly opened the door on the right for me. Inside, the car was almost unbearably hot and stuffy.

We rode in silence for a few minutes as he skillfully maneuvered through heavy traffic. I was appalled at his speed and, every so often, I pushed hard with my right foot as he came within inches of other cars. If he noticed, he was kind enough not to mention it.

After awhile he glanced at me and smiled. "Well, what do you think of Los Angeles?"

I stared straight ahead. In every lane, at every intersection all I could see were cars, trucks and vans.

"I can't help but wonder where they're all going," I said.

"Pardon? Oh! The traffic!" He laughed. "Yes, everybody in Los Angeles seems to have a car. Haven't you ever been here before?"

"Once. A long time ago, with my parents. I think I was about ten. But all I remember was going to Disneyland."

What a wonderful trip that had been! I remembered that Daddy and Mother had known some friends, and we had come from Portland on the train to visit them.

Mr. Loop glanced at me a couple of times and I guessed he was probably trying to figure out how long ago it had been. I knew I looked young for my age, and that was the reason I now wore my long, blond hair in a chignon. My complexion was pale and I had learned I could look somewhat older with a touch of rouge high on my cheek bones and with my lashes and brows accented with mascara.

"That was thirteen years ago," I said, so he wouldn't have to wonder.

"A lot has been added to Disneyland since then," he said. "I took my third grade boys out there a couple of weeks ago."

"Oh. Are you a teacher?"

"A Sunday School teacher." When he smiled, his mustache tipped sideways. "Oh, no—I could never stand to be a teacher. My hat's off to anyone who teaches."

"Me, too," I said. "My mother wanted me to be a teacher, but my dad insisted I take a business course. He was right."

"Isn't your father living?"

"No, he died when I was fifteen." I sighed and shifted slightly. "A heart attack," I added, "and then my mother died last year." I was surprised how easily I said it. I had adored my mother and sometimes even now I had a physical pain when I thought of her.

"I'm sure that's been hard on you."

"It was a shock," I agreed. "That's why I went to live with Aunt Bertha. She's been wonderful, but I'm ready now to step out on my own."

Portland held nothing for me but sad memories—but I hadn't told Mr. Loop my saddest memory. Lester, tall, blond and wonderful, dead at twenty-two in Vietnam. We hadn't been engaged. At least there was no ring. But no piece of jewelry could have made me love him more.

We had been going steady when he went overseas, and I had been as true to him as though we were married. I still hadn't had a date since I learned of his death, eight months and nineteen days ago. My heart just seemed to be lifeless. I sighed wistfully.

"Louise, we'll all do what we can to make you feel at home," Gerald Loop said. "My wife, Eunice, will have you over to dinner one night soon."

"Thank you," I said, surprised. I looked at him with new interest. Until now, he had just been a polite gentleman, providing a way of transportation. Now I realized he and his wife, and all the other church members, would soon become an important part of my life.

"What do you do for a living, Mr. Loop?"

"I'm a CPA. I guess that's the reason I'm also the financial secretary at church."

"It must take a lot of work," I said, losing interest. I had never been good at math, and figures depressed me.

"Yes, a lot of work," he said, "but I'm not complaining. I'm glad to have a part in the Lord's work."

I stared out the window and watched the stream of cars coming and going. It seemed that almost every traffic light turned red to catch us.

We rode silently for awhile; then I noticed we had turned onto a wide, curving ramp which led to a freeway. We immediately shot out into traffic and I closed my eyes, praying for safety. When I opened them, I was surprised we were still speeding along, unhurt.

"Afraid, Louise?"

"A little," I admitted. I would be glad when the trip in this racing car was over.

After about ten minutes, we left the freeway and were soon among large, impressive homes with spacious lawns and tall trees.

"This is beautiful," I remarked.

"Arboleda Heights is a beautiful town. This is the old section. There's a new section of town just beyond our church where hundreds of new four-bedroom homes have gone up in the last couple of years."

"It seems so peaceful here," I remarked.

He looked over at me and smiled wryly. "Well, yes and no. We've had lots of muggings and robberies around here lately. During the day, even."

He pulled his turn signal on and, while we waited for oncoming traffic to pass, over to my left I got my first glimpse of Arboleda Heights Christian Church and School.

I was startled and somewhat dismayed. I don't know exactly what I had expected. A neat, white church with stained glass windows? A little brick schoolhouse off to one side? I don't know. But I wasn't prepared for this mammoth, rambling, two-story red brick building. It was beautiful in an eighteenth century way.

I'm not good at judging distances, but the building sat well back from the street and must have been at least two hundred feet across the front. It had a high shingled roof, and a tall old-fashioned steeple rose out of the center. It even had a bell in it.

"Do they ring the bell on Sunday?" I asked.

"No," Mr. Loop said. We shot across the street and up the paved driveway. "They left the bell as an ornament, but the pull rope was removed years ago, before my time. It's been replaced by electronic chimes. They automatically play for ten minutes every evening."

Heavy green and yellow ivy grew on much of the building, but it was trimmed neatly around the glass-paned windows.

"The church must be a hundred years old," I said.

"Only about fifty," Mr. Loop said, and we squealed into a parking place. "The building is Georgian style, I believe."

"It's beautiful, in a—a spooky way!" I laughed nervously. My palms were sweating and I turned them up in my lap to keep from wiping them on my new dress.

"Well, I'll tell you, it seems spooky when you're working in the office alone at night," he said, and turned off the ignition.

2

Mr. Loop helped me out of the car and then hurried back to unlock the trunk. He took out my suitcases, put them on the pavement and snapped the trunk shut, all in a fast, sweeping motion.

"I hadn't thought about it before, Louise," he said, and picked up the suitcases, "but where do you plan to live?" He began to walk briskly toward the main entrance.

"Mrs. Wrightwood said I could live at the parsonage, at least for awhile."

"Is that right?" He turned to look at me with his bright, inquisitive eyes. Did he disapprove? I wished I hadn't told him. I

spryly into his car. In seconds, the little car shot out of the driveway, tires screaming.''

"My goodness—that man drives fast!" Esther shook her head and clucked. "'Course, he used to be a race driver. Lucky he never got hisself killed.''

"Was he really a race driver?" I asked, remembering our trip from the airport.

"I don't think he earned his living that-a-way, but more like a hobby.'' She leaned toward me confidentially. "Mrs. Loop told me that after he became a Christian he gave it up 'cause most of the races were on Sunday.''

She bent down and pinched some aphids off a rosebud. "I tell ya, I've never seen bugs as bad as they've been this spring.''

She straightened up and wiped her hands on the back of her skirt. "Shame on me for keeping ya standin' out here.'' She opened the screen door. "Go on in, honey.''

There was a good smell of meat and onions cooking and, as soon as my eyes adjusted, I saw a metal stairway. It was carpeted in a burnt-orange color, and there were no backs to the steps, so I could see straight through to the dining area.

The living room was also carpeted in burnt orange and there was a fireplace on the wall opposite the stairway. A comfortable looking, almost shabby couch was at right angles to the fireplace, and two fat chairs sprawled on the other side of the room. There also were several tables and lamps. The room seemed warm and friendly.

"Your room's upstairs, Miss Louise, honey,'' Esther said, and started to pick up both suitcases.

I took the biggest one away from her, "Please just call me Louise, and may I call you Esther?''

"Why, sure,'' she smiled. She started up the steps. "We'll get ya settled in, and then I'll take ya around and introduce ya to ever'body.''

She looked back to see if I was following. "I think ya'll love your room, darlin' 'cause it faces the front, and my husband—that's Mr. Van Buren—he just got through papering it a couple days ago. It's got new drapes, too.''

"You shouldn't have gone to so much trouble,'' I said and watched her big, white shoes thumping up the stairs. There was a sweet scent in her wake which I finally identified as Avon's "Cotillion."

"Oh—my, the pastor ordered it. Said you'd be homesick enough without havin' a dreary old bedroom."

When we got to the top of the stairs, she opened a door to the right, and I could see another door about halfway down the hall, and a third door at the end of the hall.

"Come on in!" She was grinning like a child, eager to show off some handcraft. "Isn't it bright and cheery lookin'?"

The room *was* lovely. The wall paper was covered with tiny orange, yellow and white flowers and bright green leaves. The open drapes were of pale gold, and the windows were so wide and clean, it was almost like having an open wall. I wondered at the work it must have taken to polish each window pane.

I moved to the windows and looked out. I could see the parking lot and the lawn that flowed down to the street and for almost a block in each direction. Tall Italian cypress trees marked the boundaries. The church and school were located in the center of a growing community, but there certainly was a great amount of privacy.

I turned around and looked at my room. The high, double bed had a gold bedspread which matched the drapes. The dressing table and chest were old-fashioned and of some kind of dark wood. Everything in the room seemed sparkling clean. In the corner by the windows, I was surprised to see a small television set. How kind and thoughtful!

The wall to wall carpeting was a strange color, neither gray nor tan. I decided when they put down the new burnt-orange carpet downstairs, they must have put the old one in here. But it was clean and soft underfoot.

"Everything's just beautiful," I exclaimed. "I've never had such a nice room."

Esther's happiness spread all over her rugged features. "Bless your heart," she murmured. "We want ya to be happy here. Now look over there. That's the bathroom that ya'll be sharing with Dickie."

The dismay I felt must have shown on my face. "Oh, don't worry about 'im, honey. He's only six and most of the time he uses his daddy's bathroom downstairs."

"Then Dickie is the pastor's—"

"—son," she finished, "and there never was a sweeter boy, no matter what some says about preachers' kids. I love 'im like m'own flesh."

She bent down and straightened a throw rug in the bathroom. "Oh, he seems a little smart-alecky sometimes, but it's only 'cause he *is* so smart."

I could see another bedroom on the other side of the bathroom. I got a glimpse of a red bedspread and a few toys on the floor.

The bathroom had massive, old-fashioned fixtures. The floor was covered with tiny, octagon-shaped white tiles. There were lots of big bath towels hanging on the racks. I detected a faint Lysol scent in the room. And there was an old-fashioned gas wall heater which I hoped I would never forget and leave burning.

"Well, Louise, would ya like to rest awhile, or do ya want to go meet the rest of the folks?" she asked as we moved back into my room.

I glanced at myself in the dressing table mirror. It seemed remarkable to me that I looked just as I had a few hours ago, in Aunt Bertha's home a thousand miles away. My hair still looked neat and, if I arched my brows just a little, I looked quite competent.

"I think I'd rather meet everyone," I said—and get it over with, I added to myself. "I'm really not a bit tired."

"Isn't it wonderful how easy it is to travel nowadays?" Esther said. She started out the door. "I remember when Mr. Van Buren and I first came here from Texas—why, it took two nights and two days by train."

We were about halfway down the stairs when she turned and looked back at me, "'Course, we had to go through El Paso and Tucson, and I'll always say we would've got here sooner if we'd gone through Amarillo and Albuquerque, but sometimes ya can't tell your man anything."

I smiled down at her and waited for her to move on. I already liked Esther Van Buren, and was sure she'd be a combination aunt-mother-friend to me—but she surely talked a lot.

She took me through the dining room and into the kitchen

where she checked on her good-smelling stew. I learned that the pastor's bedroom was at the back of the house on the first floor, and that she and Mr. Van Buren lived in a one-room apartment upstairs, next to Dickie's room.

"But we also have an outside entrance and stairway, ya see, and that way we have our privacy. But Reverend Fitzsimmons has told me—if he's told me once, he's told me a thousand times—'Esther, I want you to feel like this is your home.' So, most of the time I fix our meals all together, and about the only time we use our apartment is to sleep in. Most nights, we even watch television in here 'cause, for one thing, the set's bigger and then so many nights the pastor is out at a church meeting and wants me to be here with Dickie."

I had finally concluded the pastor was a widower, and I also now realized why Mr. Loop had seemed surprised that I would be living at the parsonage. Did he feel that it wouldn't look right? Surely, though, with Mr. and Mrs. Van Buren right in the same house, no one could find fault. And yet—I knew how quick people are to suspect the worst.

What would it be like to live under the same roof with a widower? I felt flustered and wondered why Beverly Wrightwood hadn't mentioned this fact. Was he divorced? No, I was sure the church wouldn't keep him—unless, of course, his wife had been unfaithful. I had to know.

"Esther, is the pastor—what happened to Mrs. Fitzsimmons?"

Her big mouth dropped open and her eyebrows went up. "Oh, my goodness! You don't know?"

"No, I don't."

Her face was grotesque. Her lower lip and tiny chin trembled and her eyes filled with tears. She seemed overcome with sadness, and I looked away while she fought for control. In a broken voice she said, "That poor child committed suicide."

3

I don't remember what I said, but I had a heavy foreboding, an almost overwhelming impulse to leave.

Esther stared out the dining room window, pinching at the

end of her nose with a tissue. She took off her glasses and wiped her eyes.

"How did she—where did it happen?" My voice was husky.

"She got the vacuum cleaner hose from the storeroom and hooked it on the exhaust of her little car, shut herself in—" She pointed at a big building at the back of the property, then held her rough palms up and shrugged. Her chin began to tremble again and impulsively I put my arm around her. Her big frame felt boney.

"Oh, it's been terrible 'round here," she breathed. "Been four months now and I still can't go into that garage."

She heaved a big, shuddering sigh and looked at the clock in the kitchen. "My goodness, it's almost 11:30!" She straightened her shoulders and blew her nose loudly. "If we hurry, you can meet Mrs. Wrightwood and Mr. Decker before lunch."

"Where's Reverend Fitzsimmons?" I asked.

"He had a funeral this mornin', poor man." She led me through a small utility room and out a back door that opened onto the school playground.

"It's closer to go to the school offices this way," she said, ducking under a volleyball net. The blacktopped playground was huge and square shaped. It was framed by the three inside walls of the main buildings and the big building at the back of the property.

"That building?" I said pointing, "Is that—"

"Yes, honey, that's where it happened. It's called 'Fellowship Hall.' The lower part is a store room and a three-car garage, and upstairs is the church kitchen and a great big dining room. The school uses it, too. It's got a real nice kitchen with a big gas range, and there's two sinks and lots of counter space."

We had crossed the playground and gone under an outside stairway, then through double doors into a highly polished hallway. We tiptoed past two classrooms and into a big office. It held several tables, and on one of them was a duplicating machine just like the one I had used in the law office. There was also an addressing machine and a ditto machine.

Just inside the door to the right was a big, glass-topped desk. No one was seated at the desk, but there was an open shorthand tablet standing up, and paper and carbons were in the electric typewriter. A neat stack of correspondence was in the OUT box on one corner of the desk. A pink rose in a crystal vase stood alone on another corner.

"Yoo-hoo," Esther called, knocking on the doorfacing at the same time.

A slender, glamorous woman, whose age I couldn't guess, stepped out of a doorway at the back of the room. The lettering on that door read, "Leroy Decker, Principal." As soon as she saw me, she smiled widely. She was a little shorter than I, with beautiful champagne-colored hair.

"Why—it's little Louise!" she exclaimed in a spirited voice.

This had to be my Aunt Bertha's friend, Beverly Wright-wood. She whipped off her dainty half-glasses and came directly to me with her arms out. I dutifully presented my cheek. She kissed me lightly, clasped my arms, and hugged me to herself. She smelled exotic, and the bracelets on her arms tinkled femininely. I felt like a pigeon-toed twelve-year-old beside her.

"Louise!" She stepped back and looked at me. "Do you know you look just like your Aunt Bertha did at your age!" I felt myself blushing, but I was pleased. It was good to have someone in this big city who was sort of like family. I liked her. She was so beautiful and alive. "Mr. Decker!" she summoned, the walls reverberating with the sound, "Come out and meet Louise Bridges." She smiled tenderly at me, like a doting relative.

Mr. Decker came to the door, trying to put on his coat. His hair was straight and blond, parted on the side and fluffy looking, with slightly darker sideburns. His eyebrows were much darker and heavier, and his eyes were unusually large and slightly protruding. They reminded me of Greek statues I had seen—large, heavy-lidded eyes. Their summer-sky blue color made the whites appear bluish, and his face seemed very tanned.

He stared at me frankly, with a touch of a smile. His eyes held me—I felt slightly dizzy and more self-conscious than usual.

"Well, well, Miss Bridges! Welcome!" He nodded his head, smiled broadly and came forward with his right hand extended.

I had been taught that a man was supposed to wait for a woman to offer her hand, but there was nothing for me to do but shake hands. He was just about my height, but broad-shouldered and masculine. His hand was huge, hot and dry.

For half a moment I felt intensely drawn to him, but the thought of Lester lying dead somewhere in Vietnam made me pull my hand away.

"Dear Miss Bridges," he said, with a quick bow. "We're so very glad you've come."

I felt more relaxed and smiled, "Please call me Louise."

"Can't do it," he said firmly, but a tiny smile lingered at one corner of his mouth.

"Oh, he's teasing you, dear," Beverly said.

"No, I'm not," he insisted. "You see, Miss Bridges, here at school we are all 'Miss' or 'Mrs.' or 'Mister.' It's one of the ways we teach respect of elders to the students. And so," he reached out with a ball-point pen and touched the top of my head, "I christen thee Miss Bridges."

I had to laugh. I was sure I was going to like working with Mister Decker and Mrs. Wrightwood.

Suddenly, an electric, nerve-jangling bell began to ring. When it finally stopped, Esther said, "It's lunch time. Why don't you two come on back with us and have a bowl of stew?"

"I can't, Esther," Beverly Wrightwood said. "I'm dieting this week, and besides, I've already promised Shirley I'd run some dittos for her at lunch."

"I'm not dieting," Mr. Decker said, rubbing his stomach. Then his face became serious and in a quasi-undertone he said, "Will the pastor be there, Esther?"

"I don't think so. The funeral was at eleven-thirty, and I'm pretty sure he'll go back to the family's house for awhile."

"Good!" he said, his eyes bright. "In that case, I'll be glad to have lunch with you ladies."

He put one arm lightly around Esther and one around me and we started toward the door. At his touch I stiffened, and felt my cheeks and neck redden.

"Louise, dear," Beverly said, "you come back after lunch, and if the pastor hasn't come by then, I'll show you where your desk is and take you around to meet some of the teachers, okay?"

"Fine," I said, smiling. Gently, I eased away from the principal and added, "I'm looking forward to it." And I was. Although I usually dreaded meeting people, I had a happy conviction that this job was where I belonged and I was anxious to get started.

I had forgotten about the suicide, but now, as the three of us crossed the hot asphalt of the playground, the big building at the back of the property loomed ominously.

As we entered the back door of the parsonage, Mr. Decker sniffed, closed his eyes and smiled.

"Mm-mm! What is that magnificent aroma?" He went to the stove and took the lid off the pan. "Stew! My favorite!"

"That's what ya said about the chili and beans last week," Esther said, smiling and shaking her head. "I think ya jest like to eat."

"I like to eat your cooking, fair lady." He pulled a chair out from the kitchen table and sat down. "I'm ready!"

"Oh, Mr. Decker, I think we'll eat in the dinin' room today with little Miss Bridges here and all."

"Oh, no," I said, "let's eat right here. It'll be so much simpler. Where are the dishes? Let me help."

The stew was excellent and I ate more than I thought I would. Mr. Decker said funny things all through the meal and Esther and I tittered almost constantly. I guess, though, working for the attorneys and hearing so much about the ugly side of life had made me a little cynical. In spite of how amusing and interesting Mr. Decker was, I kept wondering if he was really as happy as he seemed.

"If you don't beat all, Mr. Decker!" Esther exclaimed, throwing back her head to laugh. I could see the roof of her dentures and her own pink throat beyond.

"How on earth do ya think up all these things?" She wiped tears out of her eyes and blew her nose.

"That's what I say," I echoed. "You sound like a comedian."

He laughed and then became serious. "I've always been able to make people laugh. In fact, for about two years while I was in college, I was a disc jockey on a little radio station in Indiana. I used to wisecrack and play my guitar—"

"Really?" I was impressed. "I'd love to hear you play."

"You like music?"

"Oh, yes!"

"Then you don't want to hear me play." We laughed. "You see? It's hard for me not to make jokes. Sometimes I feel that's the only reason people want me around—to be entertained." For an instant there was sadness in his eyes.

We all heard the front door open and shut, and I caught Esther and Mr. Decker exchanging glances. I was facing the dining room and I looked up expectantly. There, filling the doorway, was Reverend Richard Simon Fitzsimmons, pastor of the church, and my new boss.

His hair was very dark and wavy, combed back and receding a little, which accented a widow's peak. His brows were heavy and black; his eyes had the piercing quality of a Rembrandt portrait. He stared at me, unsmiling.

Mr. Decker jumped to his feet. "Pastor!" He wiped his mouth with his napkin. "Good to see you. Well, we haven't eaten quite all of it." He laughed, but his eyes were no longer merry. "I'd better get back to my desk."

He patted Esther on the shoulder and said, "Good meal, Esther," and then he aimed his tremendous blue eyes at me. "Miss Bridges, if I can be of any help in your work, let me know." He saluted clownishly and went out the back door.

Esther also got up and took the principal's dirty dishes to the sink. She set a place for Reverend Fitzsimmons.

"Here, Pastor, ya sit right down. There's plenty of meat still left, and vegetables, too."

He moved slowly into the kitchen. "Well, Miss Bridges," he spoke at last, and his voice was controlled. "I'm glad you're here." He smiled with his lips, mechanically, and I saw white teeth, big and even.

"Esther, please don't fix anything for me. I had a sandwich and some cake at the Parker home." He sat down at the table and I was uncomfortably aware of his nearness. It was such a small table and he was so big.

"Just give me a cup of tea, or coffee, or whatever you have."

Covertly, I noticed a fine network of lines around his eyes. He was tremendously handsome, although his nose was slightly hooked. His skin was darkly tanned, but seemed tinged with grey. He sighed; his whole attitude seemed to be one of weariness. For an instant, I felt sorry for him. Then I remembered his wife and felt on guard.

Why had she taken her life? Had there been something about this man that had driven her to suicide? And why had Mr. Decker seemed uneasy in regard to the pastor?

My heart began to beat with heavy thuds. Maybe I shouldn't have taken this job. Was it too late to leave? I could simply stand up, thank Esther for the lunch and say, "I'm sorry, but I don't believe I can do the work after all." Before they could protest, I could run upstairs, get my suitcases, and go.

Do it, do it, my intelligence said. But my cowardly body sat there, sipping a second cup of coffee. I tried to appear nonchalant.

"Where's Dickie?" the pastor asked Esther.

"He won't be here for lunch," Esther said and sat back down at her place. "The first graders got to go on a field trip, and I fixed him a sack lunch this morning. I gave him a piece of chicken and a peanut butter sandwich, and I put in a gob of those cookies. Louise, would you like some cookies?" She jumped up and started toward the cupboard. Reverend Fitzsimmons smiled condescendingly.

As time went on, I learned that Esther made everyone eat. Eating seemed to her the solution for everything. The cookies were good, but I was too nervous and self-conscious to enjoy them. I couldn't think of things to say and I was thankful Esther had plenty to say about everything.

"I thought Harry—" she looked at me, "that's my husband, Mr. Van Buren—I thought he'd be back for lunch. He had to drive into Los Angeles to get some kind of a fittin' for a toilet in the girl's rest room. Well, speak of the—"

"Careful there, Esther," the pastor said and smiled slightly.

Harry Van Buren bustled in, big as a grizzly bear, red faced and grinning good naturedly. He took off a soiled canvas hat and wiped his forehead with his arm.

"Howdy, ever'body." He stooped and kissed Esther on the cheek. She pointed at me.

"Honey, this is Miss Bridges, and she wants us to call her Louise."

"Glad to meet you," he said and sat down at the table. His rather small eyes were blue. Tiny red veins streaked the whites. His W. C. Fields-type nose also was red-veined and I wondered if he drank. Then I was ashamed of myself for wondering.

"Anything left to eat?" he asked. Esther was at the stove, filling a bowl with stew. I looked at Harry's big, gnarled hands, with dirt under the nails and wondered if he had already fixed the toilet and whether he had washed his hands. There was a faint body odor in the kitchen now and I felt a little queasy. I turned to the pastor.

"If you'll excuse me, I think I'll run upstairs and unpack a few things." As I got up, he stood quickly. He was at least half a foot taller than I.

"Why, certainly," he said. "Why don't you rest this afternoon and we can get you started on your job in the morning?"

"I'm really not tired," I said. "In fact, I've already told Beverly I'd be back this afternoon to meet the teachers."

His eyes were cold and impersonal. Were they cold or simply listless? Perhaps lifeless described them best, I decided. They reminded me of a snake's eyes I had seen at the zoo—no feeling, just staring. I gripped my arms to keep from trembling. "Anytime you want me to start, I'll be glad to."

"Well," he looked at his watch, "why don't you plan to come to the study about three this afternoon? That will give me time to clean up my desk and hide the skeletons before you come." The slightest light twinkled in his eyes.

I nodded, tried to smile, and went upstairs.

I was trying to decide if I liked him or not when I stepped into Beverly Wrightwood's office.

"There you are," she said, smiling at me. She looked at her watch. "Hmmm. Shirley Bennett's kids go to recess in five minutes. I think we'll go there first. She's our second grade teacher, and just about your age. You'll have a lot in common."

She stood up and called out, "Roy—Mr. Decker! I'm going to take Louise around now. Will you answer my phone?"

The principal came to the door. He looked pleasant and, again, his eyes bored into mine. I had a sinking sensation somewhere inside and looked quickly at Beverly.

"Be glad to," he said brightly, "if you're not gone over five minutes."

"Oh, you!" Beverly retorted. "You'll be lucky to see us again this afternoon."

"No such thing as luck in the Christian's life," he said piously.

"Okay! It'll be a blessing if you see us again this afternoon!"

"Beverly, wait a minute," I put in. "I told the pastor I'd start at three this afternoon."

Roy's eyebrows raised and his mouth turned down slightly. "Pity," he said and waved us on.

"So he's going to make you start today?" Beverly asked.

"He suggested I wait until tomorrow." Was I defending him? "But I told him I would start whenever he wanted me to."

"Well, honey, that's just up to you." We walked along the hall. "But if it was me, I'd put it off as long as possible."

I looked at her, but her face was turned slightly away. Didn't she like Reverend Fitzsimmons? If not, why not?

We walked past an empty room. "First graders are on a field trip," she explained. "Should be getting back soon."

As we got to the next door, it banged open and a stream of children surged out—some charged to the drinking fountain, some ran to the rest rooms and others raced to the playground.

A pert, brown-haired woman a little shorter than I, stood at the door saying firmly, "Don't RUN. Ted! Walk. Slow down!" She looked up at us and smiled in exaggerated weariness.

"Welcome to Bennett's Bughouse."

"The closer it gets to summer, the wilder they get," Beverly explained to me.

"Shirley, this is Louise Bridges. You know—the one I told you about."

"Hi, Louise," Shirley said and flipped her short, bouncy hair. "I've heard all about you. What I want to know is why would a nice girl like you leave a nice place like Portland to come here?"

Beverly laughed and I tried to, but truthfully, I was beginning to wonder why I had left the security of Aunt Bertha's comfortable home and a good-paying job—even if it was dull—to come to work for a man no one seemed to like. A man who might have caused his wife to commit suicide.

As usual I was slightly tongue-tied, but Shirley's voice chirped away about some idiot parent who had read her off because her child had thrown up after lunch yesterday.

"I'll never have children, I promise you!" she said, but she

24

was laughing. Shirley Bennet was cute and funny, and I felt reasonably sure we would be friends.

She sank down on the edge of her desk and pointed to the pupils' desks for Beverly and me. "So far, what do you think of Ye Olde Arboleta School and Church?" she asked.

I squeezed into one of the small chairs, and Beverly chided, "You shouldn't put her on the spot, not yet."

"Has she met The Man?" They exchanged looks.

"Oh, yes," Beverly said and looked at her watch. "In fact, she has to go to work in half an hour."

"Really? Poor baby!" Shirley's face was contorted in mock pity. So far I hadn't said a word and Shirley continued, "Sometimes these kids get on my nerves, but I'll take them any day to what you have ahead of you, Louise."

Another innuendo. What did it mean? What was ahead?

Shirley and Beverly talked a little more, mostly about school business, we said goodbye and started back toward the office. At her door, I whispered my thanks to Beverly as she entered her office, and then walked on down the hall toward the office that would be my own.

This part of the hall was carpeted and my feet made no sound as I walked along, dreading—yet eager—to find out what my new job and my new boss would be like.

A smooth, bronze plaque read, "Pastor's Study," and I knocked timidly on the dark walnut door.

"Come in," Reverend Fitzsimmons called.

I turned the brass knob slowly. This was it. When I stepped over the threshold, I would be committed.

4

As I had imagined, my office was dark and gloomy. The arrangement was the same as Beverly's—that is, one must go through my office before entering the pastor's study. Instead of office machines, however, there were four straight-backed armchairs and two end tables, besides my desk and chair.

The study door was open and I saw the pastor seated at a

massive desk, hunched over some papers. Several open books were on the desk and he seemed to be copying something out of one of them.

At last he looked up at me. He didn't smile or frown, and I was impressed again by how lifeless he seemed to be. He was like an automaton, going through the motions expected of him, but without feeling.

"Come in, Miss Bridges. I guess I'd better call you Louise."

"I would prefer that," I said, "although Mr. Decker said I had to be 'Miss' in front of the students."

"I think that's a good policy. Most kids today don't have much respect for authority—including my own son." There was a faint sparkle in his eyes.

"I haven't met him yet."

"Dickie's not *too* bad." He smiled one sidedly. "Being the only child, I suspect he's a little spoiled."

"I'm looking forward to meeting him," I said politely, but I was uneasy about sharing a bathroom with a spoiled six year old boy.

"He'll be tearing in here any minute now, so perhaps I ought to outline your duties before he gets here. It'll be impossible once he's here."

I wondered why. Couldn't he control him, or did he mean he would stay here the rest of the afternoon? But the pastor answered my question.

"He hangs around with me a lot lately—ever since his mother went to be with the Lord." He stood up, put his hands in his pockets and moved slowly to the window. His back was to me, and, with his shoulders slumped, he looked completely dejected.

I had an impulse to go to him and offer comfort, but I remembered Shirley's remark about what I had ahead of me as his secretary and stiffened.

"I guess you've heard about Vera—about my wife."

"Yes." I felt embarrassed.

"From Esther?" He turned to face me.

"Yes."

His mouth tightened slightly. He hadn't invited me to sit down and I was standing only a few feet from him. I realized

26

again what a big and powerful man he was.

"But she didn't volunteer the information, Reverend—"

"Call me Pastor. It's easier."

"Esther wasn't gossiping. I had asked her where Mrs. Fitzsimmons was, and that's when—"

He waved his hand. "It's all right. Naturally everyone is still talking about it. It was just four months ago."

He sighed loudly and went back to his chair. Then he looked at me as though seeing me for the first time.

"Well, Louise, let me show you my filing system."

I walked around his desk and stood beside a four-drawer metal filing cabinet. When he opened the first drawer, I was impressed with its neatness. The hanging folders swung easily; nothing seemed crowded or messy.

"My wife set up this system," he said. His voice sounded wistful. "She was my secretary, and, while some husband and wife teams don't work well together, we got along fine."

He showed me where he kept his sermons, church correspondence, copies of newsletters and bulletins, information on missions, membership records, all the things that I would have to find or file.

"Now, let's go into your office and I'll explain the telephone and intercom." In my office he flipped on an overhead light and the room became a little cheerier.

My desk was empty except for a calendar which showed the current date. I wondered who had turned it. He pulled open drawers and showed me the church letterheads, envelopes and other stationery; then he snapped the typewriter into place. It was a late model IBM and I grimaced. I walked around the desk so I could see it better and almost stumbled over the cord.

"Watch out," he said. "Tell Harry to get you an extension so you can use that outlet back there." He shook his head. "I told Vera to do that. People keep stumbling over it and it's getting frayed."

I looked at the typewriter and sighed. "I hope I can type on it. I'm used to a Royal."

"My wife loved it," he said. "The spacing is a little different, I understand, but you'll get used to it."

The window, which faced the street, would be on my right

when I was seated at the desk. Somber grey-brown drapes shut out half the light and I hoped someday I could put up new ones.

The intercom was simple. Push a button to talk, release to listen. The telephone had two lines and buttons, so that either Beverly or I could take all calls.

"The telephone will probably drive you crazy," the pastor said. "Some days I spend half my time on the phone." I nodded.

"I'm really behind in my correspondence, too." He wandered back to his office. "A few of the ladies in the church have been helping Beverly with my work, but that basket," he motioned toward a brown wooden box on his desk which was heaped with an assortment of papers and envelopes, "is full of stuff that needs to be cared for. I'd like to start with that in the morning."

"All right," I said. I had followed him back into his study and we stood facing each other. My eyes focused on the overflowing box and I wondered what kinds of letters preachers had to write.

He stepped to the window again and stared out. After a moment he said, "Louise, how long have you been a Christian?"

I was startled and had to think for a moment. I felt flustered, too, and began to blush.

"I accepted Christ when I was about eight years old," I said, "at a Good News Club."

His intense eyes were boring into mine. Didn't he believe me? "But I rededicated my life when I was fifteen." He continued to stare at me for another ten seconds.

"I know I'm saved!" I said a little angrily.

"Good." He walked around his desk and sat down. When he leaned back, his chair made a loud, squawking noise. He motioned to a chair at the side of his desk.

"Please sit down and forgive my abruptness. But I wanted to be sure you are a real Christian. Many people say they are, and of course, only God really knows the heart. Usually, though, if a person can look back in his life to a time when his life changed, we can assume he is one. Not always, though."

He cleared his throat and his eyes narrowed. He picked up a pencil and turned it with both hands, then put it down.

"Louise, much of the work in this office is confidential. You are not to repeat anything you hear. Nothing hurts the work as much as gossip. So, no matter how tempted you are to share something with Esther, or perhaps Shirley Bennett or Beverly—"

"I won't, I promise." My eyes were wide open and I felt apprehensive, yet excited.

"Your hours will be roughly from 8:30 in the morning until around 5:00. Sometimes you might have to work longer. Some days, especially in the summer, you can quit when your work is done—that is if I'm here to cover the phone."

"I thought Beverly—"

"Beverly and Roy usually work morning hours during the summer, and sometimes not at all, depending on their work load." He picked up the pencil and drummed it on the desk.

"Roy's primary duty here is principal of the school, but he is also the church's associate pastor, and he sometimes takes my place in the pulpit. He's a good preacher."

The thought of the bright and charming principal came to mind and I hoped I would get to hear him preach soon.

"One other thing, Louise," he cleared his throat again. "As my secretary, I think you should be a member of this church. So it would be good to send for your church letter as soon as possible." I nodded, but I felt irritated. Shouldn't church membership be voluntary?

"And of course," he went on, "I will expect you to attend most church services."

I caught my breath. What nerve! I felt myself getting hot and angry. I loved church and had gone to everything at home, but I didn't like to be told that I *had* to be in church. I felt my jaw jut out.

"Now, I see I've made you angry," he said and leaned forward. "I'm sorry, but it's for your own reputation. You see, for awhile, as my secretary, you'll be in the limelight. I don't want anyone to find fault with you."

He looked at me in a fatherly way, and I relaxed a little. I even smiled. I'm not one to hold grudges.

"Okay," I agreed. "I'll send for my letter, and I'll be at every service, unless I'm sick."

"Good." He looked beyond me. "Well, there's old Dickie. Hi, son."

I turned and saw a thin, pale little boy, not at all like his father except for his eyes. They had the same piercing quality and right now they were aimed at me.

He walked around me suspiciously, with his tongue in his cheek, and went to the preacher. He put his mouth close to his father's ear and whispered coarsely, "Who's that?"

The pastor pulled his head away slightly and frowned. "It's not polite to whisper in front of people."

"Miss Bridges, I'd like to present my son, Dickie." The boy leaned on his father's chair arm and the pastor gently placed his big arm around him.

"Dickie, this is my new secretary. She's going to be living at our house."

"Are you going to be my new mom?" His face was innocent and his brown eyes enormous. My cheeks felt like fire.

"I just told you, Dickie. She's my secretary. Now, how about you going to see if you can help Esther?"

"But I wanted to tell you about the bakery."

"Oh, that's right. You got to go on a field trip." Richard Fitzsimmons gazed fondly at the boy and rubbed his thin little shoulders.

"Yeah! And it was so neat. They let all of us have cupcakes! Free!"

"That's great!" He gave Dickie a quick hug. "Now son, I want you to go home. I have many things to show Miss Bridges."

"Oh, no!" He flung himself out of his father's embrace and glared at me. In a whiny voice he pleaded, "I won't get in the way. Please let me stay, please?"

Reverend Fitzsimmons' eyes narrowed and his mouth became a straight line. He said in a metallic voice, "Dick, I want you to go now, without arguing."

"Okay!" the little boy shouted, his high voice breaking with anger. He stamped toward the door and then turned to give me an ugly look.

"If it wasn't for you, I could stay!" Before his father could do anything, Dickie ran out and slammed the door.

We sat silently for a moment. If he had been mine I would have dashed down the hall, grabbed him and given him a spanking.

The pastor sighed again and I looked up at him. I tried to make my face expressionless.

"I'm sorry, Louise. He misses his mother." He looked down and began to slowly open and shut one of the books. "We both miss her, and I guess I've kept him with me too much since—"

"I understand," I said, no longer disgusted. Poor little boy. "Well, after today you needn't change your routine. You can still spend your afternoons with him."

"I should change our routine. It's not good for him to spend all the time after school with me. He should be with someone his own age." He smiled then and his eyes had a momentary light in them. "Besides, I'm tired of hunting for lizards and toads."

For the second time that day I walked back across the play-ground to the parsonage. I was sure it would be closer to go across the front of the church and through the narthex, but since I hadn't seen it yet, I was afraid I'd lose my way. Besides, I was sure Esther would be in the kitchen preparing the evening meal and I didn't want to disturb her by making her answer the front door. I wondered if they would give me a key to the parsonage. I should have asked about that.

As I neared the back door, Dickie came to meet me. "Want to see my lizards?" He was smiling, and there was no trace of his ugly mood.

"I sure do," I said and smiled widely. I was relieved he wanted to talk to me.

"Come on. I keep them in my room."

I kept smiling and hoped he couldn't detect the dismay I felt. "Where do you keep them? In a coffee can?"

He looked disgusted. "Not in a coffee can. That wouldn't be big enough. I have four lizards and two salamanders, so my dad bought me a terrarium."

"Oh, good!" I said. "That way they can't get loose."

"I take them out and pet them." I tried to conceal my shudder. I would probably faint if one of the things crawled into my bedroom.

"Have you ever lost one?" I asked. His little face grew sad.

"The day my mom died I had them out on my bed and one got away and crawled into the furnace register." He looked bleak, thinner than ever.

"Well, maybe he didn't die," I said cheerfully. "He probably just scooted down the outside of the pipe and found his way outdoors again."

His face brightened a little. "That's what my dad said. I hope so."

"Dickie," Esther had come to the screen door, "don't keep Miss Bridges standin' out in the sun. You'd better get washed for supper anyhow."

Dickie and I went into the good-smelling kitchen and I saw parkerhouse rolls rising on the counter.

"Louise, honey, don't ya let Dickie wear ya to death now," Esther said. "He can talk an arm and a leg off if ya let 'im."

Dickie slouched away toward the stairs. When he was out of hearing I asked, "Esther, why is he allowed to keep lizards in his room?"

"Why, honey, the child has to have a pet a some kind. Here on the church grounds he's not allowed to have a dog and those lizards are plumb cute if ya watch 'em. Clean, too." She looked at me kindly.

"Now, I don't like the salamanders as much. Got a tail like a snake, but they are a nice hobby for the boy."

Though it was warm in the kitchen, goose bumps stood out on my arms. I'm a terrible sissy about snakes and spiders and, while I had never had an encounter with a lizard, I was sure I abhorred them.

"Well, if they ever get loose and get in my room, I'll probably throw a fit," I said, wide-eyed and emphatic.

Esther looked at me sadly. I knew she loved Dickie, and probably felt toward him like a grandmother. She spoke primly.

"I'll speak to 'im extra strong about keeping the lid fastened," she said and turned away from me. She started toward the sink. I followed her and touched her lightly.

"Oh, don't do that," I protested. "Maybe," I bit my lip, "I'll just try not to be such a baby."

Her big brown eyes behind the thick lenses softened.

"They can't hurt ya," she said. "Honest, honey, don't be 'fraid."

That night as I lay in bed, I was afraid. Not of the lizards, especially—but of the future. Why did Lester have to get killed? Why couldn't he have come back to Portland? We'd probably be married by now. And why did my mother have to die, just when I needed her so?

I felt tears forming and I didn't want to start crying. I raised up and looked out the window. If I had been in Portland, I would have seen the Johnson's house next door and the tall pine tree. Homesickness washed over me and I knew I was going to have to do something or I would cry until I had a headache.

I had sort of a headache anyway and remembered I hadn't eaten much dinner. Esther had prepared a wonderful meal—ham and beans, salad and homemade rolls. But I was still self-conscious and uncomfortable around Reverend Fitzsimmons, and I had taken a dislike to Harry Van Buren, probably because he wasn't clean about his person. At dinner he was wearing the same dirty clothes he'd had on at noon, and I had to look away from his hands to keep from feeling sick. As a result, I had only picked at my food.

Now, it was past eleven and I realized I was hungry. Esther had told me I could have the run of the house and to feel free to eat anything there was in the kitchen. I got out of bed and put on my robe, a lovely pink one Aunt Bertha had given me. It was ruffled and feminine, but long and modest.

I decided to go to the bathroom first and, when I flicked the light switch, Dickie called out, "Miss Bridges, would you come here?"

I opened the door to his room and the light from the bathroom beamed in on him. In the big bed he looked even smaller.

"What's the matter, Dickie?"

"Nothing. I can't sleep. And I'm sorry."

"Sorry?" I sat down beside him. The room smelled like

tennis shoes.

"Yeah, I'm sorry I had a tantrum."

"That's okay," I touched his arm briefly. "Dickie, why don't you sleep downstairs with your father? It seems lonely for you to be away up here, and him to be downstairs."

"Well, you see," he sat up straight in the bed and took on an air of teacher with pupil, "before my mom went to Heaven, my mom and dad both slept in your room. And then after my mom—you know—just my dad slept in there." He counted off these events on his thin little fingers.

"And then they said a sec-u-tary was coming, which is you, and Harry and Esther had to fix up the room, so my dad started sleeping downstairs in the back bedroom."

"But weren't you lonesome?"

"No, because lots of nights Harry was working on that room—and anyway I have my lizards up here."

"I wonder why they didn't have me sleep downstairs?"

"Because my dad has to be gone lots of evenings and he said it would be easier for him to have the downstairs room. It's little and dark and my dad said a girl wouldn't like it."

"Are you hungry?" I asked.

"Yeah! Are you going to eat something?" He was already out of bed, hitching at his pajamas to keep them up.

"I thought I'd make cocoa if I can find the things."

"Come on! I'll show you!"

Dickie got the cocoa and pan out for me and, although we were as quiet as we could be, Pastor Fitzsimmons came to the kitchen, dressed in a blue terrycloth bathrobe and pajamas. His hair was a little tousled and he grinned boyishly.

"What's going on?"

"We're making cocoa," Dickie said importantly. "You want some?"

"Don't mind if I do," Richard Fitzsimmons eased his big body into a chair at the table and stretched his legs. I was aware of the fact we were in bathrobes, but I pretended to be completely at ease and made myself concentrate on stirring the cocoa.

"Esther usually has some cookies," the pastor offered.

"I'll get them!" Dickie ran to yank open a bottom drawer,

34

jumped on it and bounded up on the counter. He snatched open a cupboard door and brought out a cookie jar.

I looked at the preacher, and our eyes met in an indulgent, smiling exchange. Dickie was cute, and we both knew it.

I didn't enjoy my cookies and cocoa as much as I would have if it had only been Dickie and me. The pastor was not talkative and I do not have the ability to make light conversation. I wondered if I would always be this uncomfortable with him.

I thought of Leroy Decker. Roy. My mind savored that name. How easy it had been to talk and laugh with him during lunch. Where was he at this moment? Was he married? A father?

"Where does Mr. Decker live?" I said aloud, glad to think of something to say.

"He has an apartment about a mile from here," the pastor answered. "He lives with another fellow, a teacher in one of the public schools, I believe."

He was single! This information gave me a happy lift.

"Roy will make a good husband," the pastor said and smiled at me as though he could read my mind. I looked down quickly. "Or do you already have a young man?"

"My fiance was killed in Vietnam," I said, and looked directly into his eyes. His smiled vanished.

"I'm sorry." There was a strained thirty-second silence. I picked up my cup and saucer and took them to the sink.

"Dickie, are you through?" I asked. "How about you, Pastor Fitzsimmons?"

"Don't worry about the dishes, Louise. Esther's used to finding dishes in the sink. And Louise, around home, why don't you call me Richard? Before strangers and the students, Pastor is fine, but here at home, I think it might help us to relax to be on a first name basis."

"Neato!" Dickie exclaimed. "It's kind of like having Mom here, huh, dad?"

I looked quickly at the pastor. Would I ever be able to call him Richard? He had been smiling a moment before, but now his face was blank. I knew he must be thinking of his wife. Was he comparing me with her? And finding me a poor substitute? I lifted my chin slightly.

What did I care what he thought of me? I certainly wasn't interested in him—as a man. I tried to think of Lester, but I couldn't bring his face to my mind. Neither did I feel sadness as I thought of him. Was it because I had learned tonight that Leroy Decker was single?

5

I had a hard time deciding what to wear to work the next morning. The national uniform for women was pants, but I had worn dresses to the law office in Portland and I had expected to wear dresses to work as the pastor's secretary.

Yesterday Beverly had worn a dress, but all the teachers had worn pantsuits. I wasn't as wild about clothes as some girls, but the things I had bought in the past year were nice.

Carefully, I considered everything in my wardrobe and decided to wear my navy blue dress. It was made of a light weight doubleknit, had a flared skirt and an airy white ruffle at the neck. I always felt dressed up and at ease in it.

I brushed my hair, taking extra care to get it just right. I took a hand mirror to the window to apply my makeup. I certainly didn't want to wear too much.

I felt a mixture of dread and anticipation. What would my first day as a pastor's secretary be like? I put on high-heeled white pumps and whirled around. Would I see the principal, Roy Decker? I remembered his height and quickly took off my high heels and slipped my feet into sandals. I was provoked at myself for doing this. What did it matter anyway?

My lawyer bosses had given me an expensive perfume for a going-away present and I sprayed a small amount on my wrists and neck. I slung my purse strap over my shoulder and ran downstairs.

Esther called after me when I ran out the back door.

"Honey, ya can't go to work 'out breakfast!"

But I was already on the playground. I still hadn't seen the narthex and sanctuary, but going this way, I would have to walk past Beverly Wrightwood's office.

As I had hoped, her door was open and, although she was not there, I could see Roy seated as his desk. The morning sunlight at his back seemed to make a halo around his head. He was in a blue shirt with the cuffs rolled up.

He looked up as I paused at the doorway. He grinned at me and his eyes had an inner light. "Well, good morning, glory!" he said and stood up.

He came quickly into Beverly's office. I had not intended to stop (had I?), but it was evident he wanted to talk to me. I was pleased, but held myself rigid and smiled primly.

"How nice you look," he said, eyeing me up and down. "I like to see a woman in navy blue and white. Makes her look distinguished." He lounged casually on Beverly's desk and looked at me directly.

"Well, I see you survived your first night at the manse." He lifted his left eyebrow slightly and smirked. What did he mean? Had he somehow found out about the cocoa episode? Or was he inferring that I was in some kind of danger?

He must have seen my confusion. He added in a stage whisper, "I only meant that things might be a little dull, you know," and he jerked his head in the direction of the pastor's study.

"Oh, no," I said. "Esther prepared such a good dinner, then I had to unpack, and Dickie and I got acquainted."

"What do you think of the Lord and Heir?" He rolled his eyes up meaningfully.

I laughed and started to tell him that I thought Dickie was spoiled and that I hated the idea of lizards in his room. But some inner warning made me say, "He's fine. He's really cute."

I was going to have to be careful, I thought, because there was something about Roy that made me want to confide in him. I felt I had known him for a long time. However, I got the impression that he didn't like Reverend Fitzsimmons.

I had received the same impression yesterday, first from Gerald Loop, then Beverly, and finally from Shirley Bennett, the second grade teacher.

All of them, either by a hesitation in speech or a meaningful glance, seemed to convey their dislike for the preacher. I was sure it had something to do with his wife's suicide. I felt a little afraid of him, too, and honestly wondered if he had been the reason she had felt life was no longer worth living.

But as I remembered him last night, drinking cocoa with Dickie and me, hair tousled and feet bare, I couldn't imagine him in any sort of dreadful role. Whatever the pastor was, right now he was my boss, and I owed him my loyalty.

I looked at my watch and gasped. "It's quarter to nine! I've got to run!"

I felt miserable going to work fifteen minutes late on my first day, and I was glad to see the door to his study was closed. He was in there, though, because I could hear his voice. He was either talking on the phone or had a client—client? No, that's what they were in the law office. Inquirer? I'd have to find out, but right now I was relieved I wouldn't have to explain why I was late.

I went quickly to my desk, put my typewriter up into place and sat down. I looked around the desk's surface and wondered what I should do. I turned the calendar to April 2, pulled open the center drawer and looked at the pencils (all sharp), paper clips and rubber bands.

In the top drawer on the right, I found a steno pad. "Vera Fitzsimmons" was written on the cover. I took it out slowly, with the guilty feeling that I was reading someone else's mail. Still, I reasoned, if he hadn't wanted me to see it, it wouldn't be here, would it?

As I held it, it seemed gruesome to me that the person who had used this book was dead. I started to put it back, then slowly opened it. The pages were covered with shorthand outlines. Neat outlines, beautiful. In fact, they were so good I could read her shorthand easily and proceeded to read several letters.

I lost track of time, thoroughly engrossed in deciphering and reading the pastor's letters. I was surprised when I turned a page to find a note written in longhand. I quickly looked back at the cover and compared Vera Fitzsimmons' signature with the words in the note. I was sure it was the same hand.

The note was evidently a first draft to one of the church members:

Dear Eunice:

I'm sorry to do this, but I don't know what else to do. I'm swamped with Junior Church, working for Richard and trying to be a mother to Dickie. I simply cannot take on VBS next summer and I was won—"

At this point, she had slashed through all of it with her pen. On the next page, she had tried again. "I'm sorry to do this, but I don't know anyone else who is qualified. Do you think you—" Again, she had crossed it out.

That was the last thing in the notebook. I felt sorry for Vera Fitzsimmons. I knew what it was like to have too many jobs in the church. But surely that wasn't the reason she took her life. There had to be another reason.

Had Richard Fitzsimmons driven her to this point by making her take part in everything? He seemed considerate to me, but I had only been here a little over twenty-four hours. In that time, he had grilled me about my beliefs and practically ordered me to be at all services. He claimed he didn't want a hypocrite to be his secretary, so it didn't seem likely that he would be one. Yet, his devout manner could just be a front.

Without warning, the study door opened. I jammed the steno pad back in the drawer and turned around. A slender, beautiful woman came out of the study. She was as tall as I, and her hair was frosted—a fad I had wanted to try, but Aunt Bertha had talked me out of it. On this woman, it was startling and extremely chic.

She was dressed in a simple white dress, sleeveless and low-necked. Wherever her skin was exposed, it was smooth and tanned. She looked and walked like a model, and as she came toward me, I could smell a lovely scent. I couldn't guess her age. She could be anywhere from twenty-five to forty. She was completely self-possessed, except there was faint evidence she had been crying. Her nose and the rims of her eyes were pink. She touched her nose delicately with a lacy handkerchief.

Richard also looked disturbed. He was frowning, but he seemed more handsome this morning than I had remembered him. He was dressed in a tan sports coat and his white shirt seemed brilliant next to his dark face. His brown slacks had a sharp crease in them, and he looked as important and commanding as my attorneys. He smiled at me stiffly.

"Vanessa, I'd like you to meet our new secretary, Louise Bridges," he said. "Louise, this is Vanessa Hamilton, one of our members."

Vanessa turned her head and smiled with her lips.

"Hello, Louise." Her voice was low and genteel, but her eyes were cold and wary—and I received the immediate impression she looked down on me, perhaps didn't approve of me. But there I was, judging! We hadn't even gotten acquainted. Maybe she was just embarrassed, because no woman likes to meet someone for the first time when her eyes and nose are red from crying.

I smiled at her, murmured, "Hello," and turned back to the typewriter, pretending to be busy. I watched her as much as I could without appearing to stare.

She turned her attention to Richard. "Thanks for seeing me this morning." Her aquamarine eyes when focused on Richard were suddenly warm. She stood so the light from the window was full on her face and I could see her expression. Her full lips were slightly parted and she looked up at him wistfully. With a pink-polished finger, she touched his sleeve.

"See you tomorrow night." She whirled around, ignored me and walked out of the office with her head high.

Richard watched her go, then turned to me, "Sorry I wasn't free when you came in."

"That's all right," I smiled at him, "I was a little late."

"I had planned to tackle that mess on my desk, but I have two important letters I'd like to give you. Let's try to get them in this morning's mail." He started toward his office. "You'll find a notebook in the desk, I believe."

I picked up the half-used steno pad and followed him. I could feel beads of perspiration break out on my forehead. What if I couldn't take his dictation? But I needn't have worried. He was concise, knew what he wanted to say, and yet wasn't too fast.

Later, at the typewriter, it was a good feeling to be able to transcribe my notes. However, it took me over an hour to do

40

the letters, primarily because I wasn't used to the typewriter and had to type one of the letters over.

I held my breath as he read them slowly and carefully. It was a relief when he picked up his desk pen and signed them. I was just sealing the envelopes when the mailman came in.

Richard came out of his office and reached for the mail. "Hi, Jerry," he said pleasantly.

"How do, Reverend," Jerry said. His eyes were round and dark. He was short and heavy, and his head was too big for his body.

"Jerry, this is Miss Bridges. She's my new secretary."

"Pleased to meet you," he said. His eyes were soft and friendly.

Richard looked at him and drew a deep breath. "Jerry, we're having a Men's Fellowship next Monday night." Jerry looked down and busied himself with the mail. "They're serving barbecue beef and beans, and I'll treat you if you'll come."

"Well, I'll check with the missus," Jerry said apologetically. "Sure is gettin' hot out." He took off his blue helmet and wiped his head.

"Is it?" Richard seemed to lose interest and flipped through the mail. He tossed it all on my desk. "Most of this stuff can go in File 13."

He grinned at me and Jerry shrugged, "Don't think I like all that junk mail." He shook his heavy head. "Glad to have met you, Miss Bridges."

After he left, Richard stood at my desk and picked at a couple of envelopes.

"Open all of it," he told me, "and do what you think best." He turned and started toward the door.

"I'm leaving now. If anyone needs me, you can reach me at the Manhattan Restaurant. There's a ministerium luncheon today." He was almost out the door. "I should be back by 1:30." He waved vaguely and disappeared.

He hadn't given me any work to do except to open the mail, and I felt confused and lonely. I glanced at my watch and was amazed to see it was already 11:30. I didn't know what to do about lunch. He hadn't given me an office key and I was sure he wouldn't want me to leave without locking up. I was beginning to feel a little angry with Reverend Fitzsimmons, when Roy knocked on the open door.

"Miss Bridges?" He clicked his heels together and bowed. I laughed. "Would you be kind enough to go to lunch with me?"

"How nice of you!" I exclaimed. "But I don't think I can go any place for lunch until the pastor comes back."

"Nonsense! Now's the time to go. When he comes back you can't go because you'll have to work." He came over to my desk and sat on the corner of it. He was too close and it made me self-conscious and happy at the same time.

"Where is he, by the way?"

"He went to, ah, mini—min—"

"Ministerium. Oh, sure, it's always the first Tuesday of the month."

"What is it?"

"Ministers of the district get together to eat and gossip."

I laughed. "Shame on you!"

"It's true. Only they call it ministerium." He reached over and took my left hand. I was startled and drew back.

"Relax!" he said. "Just looking at that ring."

I looked down at the opal in an old-fashioned setting.

"It was my mother's."

"Just wanted to be sure it wasn't a diamond," he said lightly. "Well, if Richard is at ministerium, he won't be back until at least 1:30. No reason why I shouldn't take you to lunch—at McDonald's." He stood up and stretched. "While the good pastor is eating swiss steak and mashed potatoes, we'll have a hamburger."

"How do you know what he'll eat?"

"Oh, I've been to ministerium. Didn't you know that the principal of this school is also an ordained minister?"

"That's right!" I exclaimed. "I remember the pastor said sometimes you take his place on Sundays."

His flippant attitude vanished and, for a moment, I thought he looked angry.

"Not as often as I'd like. The old boy guards his sacred desk like a German shepherd."

"Old boy!" I was shocked. "He isn't old, and besides, he's a

42

minister of the gospel and we're to respect him."

"Well, now"—his voice rose and fell like a roller coaster, "we have a Puritan in our midst!" He smiled without humor. "So—do you eat hamburgers with me or not?"

"I don't see how I can leave. He hasn't given me a key."

"No problem!" Roy took out a bulging leather key case. "I have a key to just about every door in the place. So you see, fair maiden, I can let you in when we return." His blue eyes met mine for a dizzying moment.

"By the way," he said seriously, "do keep all doors locked, even if you're just going to be gone a few moments. Bev had her typewriter stolen last year. There seems to be an epidemic of daytime thefts."

I nodded solemnly and wondered how anyone could be blasphemous enough to walk into a church in broad daylight and steal a typewriter.

"Well, let's go." He stood back to let me walk through the door, then locked it. "I have a car, but it's only a couple of blocks to McDonald's. We'll walk; it'll be good exercise."

At lunch, I kept looking in his eyes and forgetting what we were talking about. In fact, I acted absolutely idiotic. I giggled like a teen-ager at everything he said. There was something hypnotic about his eyes, and he was so charming and alive! I finally made myself behave.

"Where were you born, Roy?"

"Born? I wasn't born. Just hatched."

"Oh, that's horrible," I said and wrinkled my nose. "Corn."

His smile faded then, and he looked away from me.

"I was born in a little town in Indiana. You can't find it on a map. My folks were farmers. I hated the farm, so right after high school I got away. After bumming around for awhile, I went to work for a radio station in Indianapolis. I told you that yesterday."

"Why did you quit radio? It seems like such an exciting life."

"I got fired." He looked glum. He picked up a limp French fry and ate it thoughtfully. "It was just as well. By that time, I had worked my way through college and getting fired was the kick I needed to make me start seminary."

He wiped his mouth with a paper napkin, wadded it up and dropped it on the paper-covered tray. He looked so dismal I decided never to bring up the subject of radio again. He stood up.

"We'd better get back. Us peons only have half an hour." I gulped the last of my cola. His mood continued to be gloomy as we walked back to school.

"What's wrong, Roy?" I asked.

His mouth turned down sarcastically. "Oh, it's just that whenever I think about getting fired I realize what a second-rater I am. Always an also-ran, never a winner."

"You're so old, too," I said.

"I'm thirty, and that's not young. I've really made a mess of things. You see, it's the pattern. It won't change. In high school, I just missed being elected Head Boy. In college, I almost had a good enough average to graduate 'cum laude.' "

I was embarrassed and disturbed. I didn't know what to say, and I was dismayed at this side of the principal. We didn't know each other well enough for him to be baring his thoughts this way.

"Yep." He said it meaninglessly. He started to walk faster—almost as though he had forgotten me. "I've really messed it up."

"I'm sure you haven't made a mess of anything," I said breathlessly.

"You're right! *I* probably haven't. But I have been the victim of the wierdest combination of events. If a person was allowed to question God, I would have to question why I am the principal of a second-rate school, and someone like Reverend Richard Fitzsimmons is head man on the totem pole."

We were almost running now. "What do you mean—someone like Richard?"

He glanced at me but didn't answer. We walked in silence for a few moments; then he slowed his pace.

"Louise, please, please forgive me. And this is your very first day."

I looked at him and he looked so sad I spoke quickly, "It's okay; I just wish I could help."

"Dear, sweet little innocent," he murmured. "It's wicked of me to burden you with my problems. But it isn't just my problem. There are others, important people in the church."

"Pardon?"

"It's just that—well, these things concern everyone in the church family."

"What are you driving at, Roy?"

"Ah, Louise. I'm not one to gossip, but you'll hear it sooner or later. It's a matter of honesty. A sum of money—not an enormous amount, but quite a large sum of money—was taken awhile back from the church safe."

He looked at me carefully as we walked along, now almost strolling. I took a deep breath and, whether it was smog or my emotions, I couldn't seem to get enough oxygen. I turned to him.

"But you said there had been many thefts—"

He shook his head sadly.

"No, dear. This couldn't have been a theft such as Beverly's typewriter. You see, only two people in the church can open the safe. It's not a combination lock, and only two people have keys."

He stared at me and I felt he was trying to make me understand without saying the words, but—what on earth was he trying to tell me?

He stopped walking and faced me. He put his hand lightly on my shoulder and looked into my eyes. It was as though he had to tell me of a death in the family.

"Louise, the pastor, Richard Fitzsimmons, and Gerald Loop, the financial secretary, are the only two people in the church who have keys to the safe."

He waited for that to register. "Mr. Loop is a rich man." He took my arm and pulled me along gently.

"And then," he continued, "there's the matter of his wife. Have you heard about Vera Fitzsimmons?" I nodded. "Well, why did she kill herself? Don't you see, he must have made her life miserable. Or—did she know he had stolen the money from the safe?"

6

We walked the rest of the way in silence. I was frightened and appalled by what Roy had said about Richard. How could I stay and work for a man who might be a thief?

And why *did* Vera commit suicide? A picture came to my mind of Richard Fitzsimmons, towering over a meek little wife, shouting at her, commanding her to attend every meeting, forcing her into Christian service. He had made me understand I was to attend every service. Maybe his religious zeal was actually a cover-up. But something inside rebelled at this thought.

We were inside the school grounds when I said, "You know, Roy, it's hard for me to believe these things about Reverend Fitzsimmons. He's been so nice to me."

Children were everywhere, some eating out of sack lunches, others playing. "Hi, Mr. Decker!" they called out, over and over. The children didn't know me yet and many stared rudely.

Roy didn't comment and I went on. "Dickie told me the reason he gave me the nicest bedroom upstairs and took the small room for himself was so I would be happy."

He still didn't answer, so I didn't speak again, either. When we got to my office, he unlocked the door and, as he flipped the key back in the case, he straightened and looked at me.

"Louise, try to forget what I said. I have no right to try to influence you, no matter what I think."

"But the money was stolen," I said, wanting to be fair.

"Yes, but after all, too many good men have been hung on circumstantial evidence." His manner was sincere and almost repentant. He seemed eager to have me believe him. I felt sorry for him, but I was also relieved. I didn't know either man well enough to take sides.

"Roy, has anyone tried, I mean really tried, to find out who took the money?"

He frowned. "What do you mean, try? There are two keys; the safe wasn't damaged—"

"Why couldn't it have been Mr. Loop?"

"The main reason was because he was at Palm Springs when it happened."

"What does the pastor say?"

"He denied it. Said he'd be glad to put it back from his own money, but the Board of Deacons wouldn't hear of it."

"Could there have been an error in counting?"

He grunted with disgust. "That's what they've decided to call it," Roy shrugged and raised his eyebrows, "rather than have an investigation. But—" His eyes flicked back and forth and then focused on mine.

I found myself hypnotized again by this special look between us. He reached out and took my little finger.

"Forgive me?"

"There's nothing to forgive," I said, as I felt a sinking sensation in my stomach. I smiled, but I could feel the corner of my mouth tremble.

"Better get back to my duties," he said huskily. Was there something I could say to detain him?

"Roy, do you know Vanessa Hamilton?" He let go of my finger and rolled his eyes up wickedly.

"Hey, hey, hey! The lovely 'widder' Hamilton." He waved his hand in a trembling gesture. "Do I know her! She's one of our parents. Has a daughter in second grade."

"She was in to see the pastor this morning," I said. "She is so beautiful. Did you say she is a widow?"

"Yes. Her husband died a couple of years ago."

"What a shame. She's so young to be widowed."

"Probably not as young as you think. Anyway, she's rich."

"Is she nice?"

"What do you mean, nice?"

"Well, I don't know. I just sort of felt . . . oh, I don't know what I mean. Maybe—she seemed uppity."

"I think she has always had plenty of money, and people with money unconsciously exude a certain snobbishness, but I don't think she means to."

"Is she a Christian?"

"Of course she's a Christian. She's a member of the church."

47

"I know she is. But I wondered if she's a real Christian. You know—"

He stared at me as though trying to understand what I meant. He pursed his lips and made a little whistling noise.

"I wouldn't know," he said finally. "That would be judging, wouldn't it?"

I felt chastised and began to blush.

"I've got to get back," he said. "Thanks for having lunch with me." His mood had changed again and he seemed aloof.

"Thanks for inviting me." My eyes tried to meet his, but he had turned away.

I watched him walk down the hall until he turned in his office. He looked back at me and I was embarrassed for watching him. He grinned and waved.

When would I learn not to judge others, I scolded myself and sat down. But *was* Vanessa Hamilton a Christian? My mother and Aunt Bertha and I used to talk freely about whether or not we thought a person was genuine, but Roy had seemed offended when I asked his opinion about the widow. Since Roy was the principal in a Christian school, and also associate pastor, shouldn't he be interested in whether or not a person had had a real conversion experience? Maybe I was too frank and nosy. But hadn't he been more than frank with me when he talked about the pastor?

There wasn't much time to think about these things before Richard came back. As usual, he seemed detached, a man going through the motions. He gave me a couple of short letters and some sermon notes to type and then closed the door to his study.

What kind of man was behind that door? I shivered slightly as I thought of him. A cruel tyrant? A thief?

The phone rang shrilly and it was like a knife slashing through me.

"Reverend Fitzsimmons' office," I said in my most professional voice.

"May I speak to him, please?" a cultured, feminine voice answered.

"May I tell him who's calling?"

There was a pause.

"This is Vanessa Hamilton, Louise."

I was surprised at my reaction. My jaws tightened and I felt my pulse beating in my throat. For no concrete reason, I disliked this woman. In just those few words she had made me feel like a moron and a servant. I wanted to hang up on her, but instead I said, "Oh, yes, Mrs. Hamilton. Just a moment."

I pushed the intercom button, "Vanessa Hamilton, Pastor." I heard him pick up the phone.

"Yes, Vanessa?" Did I imagine he sounded irritated? I wanted to listen, but I didn't.

I learned as the weeks sped by that Vanessa Hamilton called the pastor almost every day. She also came to see him at least once a week, and often more.

She always had a legitimate reason. Sometimes it was to have him okay a letter she had written for the Christian Education Board (she was a member), or to show him a poster she had made for Women's Missionary Society (she was secretary), or to share cookies she had made for some school affair (she was room mother). She was always perfectly attired for the occasion. Never overdressed, but flawlessly beautiful. There was always an exotic scent about her and she made me feel juvenile and awkward. She was at every church service and, even though I disliked her, I had to admit she certainly seemed to be a devout Christian. This made me feel especially ashamed for not liking her.

Like her or not, of one thing I became certain. She was in love with the preacher. I had no way of knowing if he responded because any bits of conversation I overheard were always about the work of the church. His manner toward her was always the same—composed, gentle and seemingly impersonal.

I began to watch his eyes when he was with her to see if there was a special light in them, but he was always the same.

On the other hand, Vanessa came alive in his presence. Always beautiful, when Richard was near, it was as though she had been plugged in to a strong current. I wondered—and was ashamed of myself—how long she had been in love with him. Before Mrs. Fitzsimmons took her life? Before her own husband died?

I knew, as women seem to know these things, that she was conniving to get Richard. I shouldn't have cared, and I didn't care because I wanted him, but it sickened me to see her stalk him. By the time I had been his secretary four weeks, she had become more open and possessive. She would just happen to sit by him at the church dinners, or at the Sunday evening sings.

"Well, what's wrong with that?" the second grade teacher, Shirley Bennett, said one evening at dinner in her apartment. "It's legal. They're both single. Anyway, they deserve each other." She wrinkled her nose and shrugged.

Her remark didn't set well with me. I put my fork down and blotted my lips. Roy had never mentioned the stolen money again, but the thought of it was always at the back of my mind, heavy and ugly like an old vine that needed to be trimmed back. I decided right then that even though my relationship with Shirley had always been light and fun, I had to find out if she knew anything specific about Richard.

"I don't know what you meant by that, Shirley," I began. My voice sounded strange to me. "I keep hoping I am imagining it, but it seems to me you're always saying things like that."

"Like what?" Shirley asked, and helped herself to more of her good lasagna. I was always glad when she invited me to her apartment for dinner, because she was entertaining to be with and an excellent cook.

"So often, it seems to me, you and Beverly and even Roy say extremely harsh things about the pastor."

"You're kidding!" she said with mock innocence. "Have you noticed that, too?"

"Come on, Shirley. I work for him and he has never done anything wrong that I can see. At home, he seems to be a model father to Dickie. So what's wrong with him? I feel I have the right to know."

She frowned and tossed her thick hair away from her face. She looked at me levelly, her eyes wide and honest.

"To tell the truth, I don't know anything against him, personally, except that he isn't too interested in the school."

"He is, too!" I spoke quickly. "He's even writing an article on the benefits of starting a Christian School."

Shirley looked impressed. "Really?" she said. She looked down at her plate. "All I know, Louise, is what Roy and Beverly have told me."

"And what's that?"

"They seem to feel—" She jumped up suddenly. "You're out of tea!"

"Shirley! I don't want any more and don't change the subject. What do they seem to feel?"

"Oh, you! I hate to be a talebearer. If I tell you what they've told me, then I'll have to confess to the Lord I'm a gossip."

"You mean what you're going to say is gossip?"

"No. But you know we are to 'let no corrupt communication proceed out of your mouth, Ephesians 4:29.' That was the Bible verse I taught my kids last week."

"I don't want to be the cause of your sinning," I grinned at her, "but frankly, I can't see any difference in your telling me what they said about the pastor, than always cutting him down."

She looked flustered and I could hear her foot tapping. "Oh, all right. I'll tell you. It's all going to come out someday anyhow." She took a deep breath and held it a moment.

"Roy believes Reverend Fitzsimmons stole money out of the floor safe."

I shrugged. "He told me that, too."

Her mouth opened and shut and she snorted, "Then why all this third degree?"

"I guess I wanted to know what you think."

Her brown eyes hardened and she sucked in her cheeks.

"I personally think he did it." She picked up her paper napkin and absentmindedly made fringe along one edge.

"Mr. Loop and the pastor are the only ones who have a key to the safe. Mr. Loop is practically rich, so why would he want to steal? Besides, he was out of town."

"But, Shirley, why would the pastor steal? He's too intelligent." Shirley looked at me and shrugged. "No matter how strapped he was," I went on, "he wouldn't steal money in such a stupid way."

"I agree, except, maybe he didn't think he'd get caught. He

51

probably thought he could put it back on pay day."

"How much money was it?"

"A hundred dollars."

"A hundred dollars?" I sniffed. "Why he could steal that much in offerings that come through the mail addressed to him."

"Maybe he appropriates them, too," Shirley said and looked at me slyly.

"Oh, Shirley! He turns all that stuff over to me. I give any money that comes in to Mr. Loop when he comes to make the bank deposit."

She went to the kitchen and brought in a German chocolate cake.

"Oh, no!" I moaned. "Lasagna, and now this!"

"What are you crying about, you skinny thing?"

"I may be thin right now, but I have to watch it. Fat runs in my family." Shirley cut two huge pieces, scooped up a piece of coconut frosting and popped it in her mouth.

"Back to our gruesome subject," she said, and licked her fingers. "There's also a lot of talk going on about his wife. Almost everybody thinks there has to be something wrong with a marriage if one of them is driven to suicide."

"And what does the general consensus, spelled g-o-s-s-i-p, seem to be?"

She ignored my sarcasm. "Everybody thinks it was his fault."

"Esther doesn't."

"Esther doesn't see anything wrong in anybody."

"Esther told me there was a note, but she couldn't remember exactly what it said."

"I suppose the police have it. I don't remember either, but it implied she was desperate."

"What did the pastor do, when they first—you know—when it happened?" I asked.

"That's another thing. He didn't react. He even preached the following Sunday. A lot of people don't think he was sorry, because no one has ever seen him act sad, or shed a tear." She ate the rest of her cake and whittled another small piece. "He's a strange man, Louise."

"Maybe so, but his sermons are wonderful," I countered. "I've learned more in the four Sundays I've heard him than I did all winter back home."

"Yes, I agree he's a wonderful preacher, and I used to listen to every word he said, but anymore—" she frowned. "I can't believe what he says."

"I still say he's too intelligent to steal money in a way where he would be sure to be caught."

I could feel my mouth tighten and my chin lift. "You know, Shirley, I think I'm going to set my head to get the facts." She stared at me, her face a big question mark. "I know I may be wrong, but I believe he's honest." My voice was almost defiant.

Shirley's brown eyes softened. "More power to you," she said, "and I hope you're right. But I've gone over it in my mind, and Beverly and I have discussed it so many times. There's just no way the safe could be opened without a key."

"Isn't it possible that Mr. Loop or the pastor gave their keys to someone—say, when they went on vacation?"

She shook her head and closed her eyes.

"Mr. Loop hasn't left town except the weekend it happened, and Reverend Fitzsimmons hasn't been anywhere since Conference last August."

I sighed. "It does look bad for Richard." I looked up quickly. "The pastor. But I'm going to keep my eyes open and try to solve this thing. My intuition tells me he wouldn't do such a dumb thing."

Shirley tilted her head to one side and looked at me coyly.

"Hey!" she cried and smiled wisely. "You wouldn't be falling for old Fitzie, would you?"

"Don't be silly," but I could feel myself blushing. Not because of Richard, but because of Roy. So far, I hoped I had kept my feelings for him hidden. Roy and I had never had a real date, but he'd taken me to lunch a few times, and he managed to come to my office almost every time Richard was gone. He hadn't said anything special to me, but his eyes, when they locked in on mine, told me he cared.

There were other things, too. My hair, for example. Because Roy suggested it, I began wearing it down around my shoulders again. He often took a strand in his fingers and tickled my nose with it.

And another day, he put a big dandelion bloom and a lollipop on my desk with a note that read:

"Flowers and Candy to the World's Most Beautiful Lady
                                                    An Admirer"

I laughed out loud when I read it, and he stepped into the office and bowed from the waist. It was a silly thing, but it thrilled me, and that night I pressed the dandelion in my Bible.

I had never acknowledged it to myself, but I guess I had fallen in love with Roy Decker. But I didn't want to think about that now.

"No, I haven't fallen for the preacher!" I snapped, but I smiled at her. "But, Shirley, the pastor has been exceptionally nice to me, and I actually like him—I think!"

She nodded thoughtfully.

"Besides," I went on, "I think he does show his grief over his wife by being stoic."

"Could be," Shirley said, and got up. We began to clear off the table.

"And anyway, Shirley, if I was wild about him, it wouldn't do me any good. Vanessa Hamilton has her hooks in him."

Shirley leered at me. "Everybody knows that, too." She stood on tiptoe to put the cake up on the refrigerator. "But just as I told you, they deserve each other."

"Okay, Shirley," I said smoothly, but I was angry. "I'm going to prove you're wrong about my boss."

"Well, good friend, I hope you're right. It would be wonderful if somehow it turned out he is innocent. But, with everyone talking against him, I'm sure he won't be called for another year in the October meeting."

We washed and dried dishes for a few minutes without talking, each of us locked in our own room of thoughts. Subconsciously, I noted and admired Shirley's housekeeping as I put dishes away in a neat cupboard, and silverware in an orderly drawer. But my mind was really on Vanessa. I don't know why I was so against her, because from outward appearance, she was an ideal church member.

54

She served on several committees, and was always willing to do her share and more. There was no reason to believe she wasn't a good mother either, although I hadn't been around her much when she had Tammy with her. Tammy was in second grade and was always well-mannered and obedient. She was a pretty child, and her hair and clothes were always neat and clean. But I didn't like Vanessa!

"Shirley," I paused and bit my lower lip.

"Ye-es-s?" Her eyes twinkled at me.

"Do you think Vanessa is a real Christian?"

Her eyes grew wide and serious. "Ephesians 4:29," she quoted.

I wrinkled my nose and stamped my foot. "Oh, Shirley!"

She shook her head.

"I know we're not to judge people," I said, "and yet the Bible says 'by their fruits ye shall know them.'"

"Judging by her fruits, we'd have to say yes, she is a Christian, wouldn't we?"

"The Bible doesn't say we'll know them by their *works*," I retorted.

"Yes, it does! In James." She grinned at me. "Anyway, what have you got against her?" She stopped scouring the sink to look at me. "I don't feel close to her, either, but what makes you dislike her so?"

"I don't know," I said and bit my lower lip. "It's just a feeling."

"We're not supposed to go by feelings!" she teased.

"I know," I admitted, "but I remember going someplace with my parents, up in the mountains, and for some reason there were no birds in that area. There were funny buildings that looked okay on the outside, but when you tried to walk around in the rooms, you couldn't keep your balance and it made you feel sick. There was something wrong, but we didn't know what. That's how I feel about Vanessa."

Shirley lifted her brows and shrugged. "Have you ever prayed for her?" she asked.

I began to blush. "No."

It was quiet in the neat little kitchen. I thought of Jesus' words, "Pray for them which despitefully use you . . ." and I knew Shirley was right. But I didn't know if I could bring myself to pray for Vanessa.

Shirley touched my arm with a damp hand.

"I'm sorry, Louise. That was a pious, uncalled-for remark." Her eyes looked like a worried puppy, and at that moment I felt closer to her than ever before.

"That's okay," I said. "I deserved it. I don't know why I'm so gossipy tonight." I smiled at her and winked. "But—as long as I am," we both laughed, "tell me what you think of Roy."

She rolled her eyes up and twisted her mouth to one side.

"You mean as a principal or a man?"

"Both." I spoke lightly, but I felt a catch in my throat.

"I think he is a great principal. And I speak from experience. After all, I taught two years in the public schools."

"Why is he great?" I wanted to hear every detail.

"The main thing, I think, is he knows his business. He knows the teachers' problems and does everything he can to make it easier for us. Of course, he's hamstrung budget-wise. There's never enough money." The school budget didn't interest me.

"What do you think of him as a person?" I asked.

"He's nice."

"Have you ever dated him?" I held my breath and hoped my face didn't reveal how I felt.

"Oh, not really. We've had lunch together a few times, and once he picked me up to attend a session at a teachers' convention in Long Beach, but we've never had a real date."

She dried her hands and pushed the button on a hand lotion dispenser. She rubbed her hands together and the pleasant scent reached me. "He's not my type, to be honest, so I've never encouraged him—and besides he has pretty strict rules about teachers dating."

I let out my breath carefully. At least Shirley wasn't interested in him romantically.

After I went to bed that night, I lay awake for a long while thinking about Roy and everyone else I'd met in the past few weeks. I thought about Vanessa and Shirley's admonition to pray for her. Was she a Christian or not? And why did I care? In my heart before God, I knew I wasn't concerned for her soul. That admission made me so ashamed, I began to earnestly pray for her, and asked God to forgive me as well.

I finally drifted off to sleep, still trying to pray for her when I was awakened by the ringing of the church chimes. I raised up on my elbow and listened to them bonging and clanging, "Sweet Hour of Prayer."

It was so dark outside I could barely make out the shape of the window. I turned on the table lamp and looked at my watch. Three seventeen. Why were they ringing now? I knew the bells were supposed to be a Christian testimony in the neighborhood and a source of comfort. But the deafening, slightly off-key clangor was eerie in the blackness—not comforting, but terrifying.

7

A door slammed downstairs and I snapped off the lamp and ran to the window. Light suddenly flooded the side of the yard, then lights came on in the sanctuary. In less than a minute, light glimmered faintly through the vents in the bell tower. As suddenly as it had started, the chimes stopped their clanging. I watched the lights go out in reverse order and then heard the door close downstairs. I decided it had been Richard, rather than Harry, who had stopped the bells.

Everything was quiet. I stood there a while longer and wondered if the clamor had awakened Dickie, but there was no sound from his room. I got back in bed and laid there for what seemed an hour, every nerve tingling. Finally, I went back to sleep.

The next morning Richard called me into his office.

"I'm sure you heard the commotion last night," he said, smiling apologetically.

"I did!" I grinned at him. "What happened?"

"I don't know. I guess there was a short. I've disconnected the system and called the company to come check it out." He stood up. "Matter of fact, I'd better show you how to get to the tower in case I'm not here when they come."

He walked past me into my office. I followed him out the door and down the hall that led to the narthex.

The narthex was wide and spacious. It was carpeted in royal blue and paneled in dark wood, and there were two huge library tables, one on each side of the outside entry. Neat stacks of literature, flower arrangements and books were arranged decoratively on the tables. Through the stained glass windows the morning sun gave the area a pleasant atmosphere.

Across from the tables, next to the double doors that led to the sanctuary, was an ornate tract rack, well stocked with colorful tracts and pamphlets. Next to the rack was a small door I had never noticed.

Richard took a ring of keys from his pocket, selected a small dark one, and opened the door. Narrow wooden stairs faced us and Richard started up first.

We came to the first landing and reversed direction to climb the second landing. The stairwell was narrow and the plastered walls, which had never been painted, seemed to press in on me. I looked up when we got past the second landing to see sunshine filtering through the wooden slats of the bell tower. Richard's feet looked huge on the narrow steps and his tall, athletic body filled the well-like passage.

At the top, there was about a ten foot square space. On a plain wooden bench there was a record player and a stack of records. There were four old-fashioned speakers and a network of wires strung around the small room. Everything was covered with dust, except for a few footprints Richard had made the night before.

"Where are the bells?" I said and squinted up at the top of the tower.

"There are no bells," he said, "except the old one you can see from the outside. Just these records." He hunched his shoulders and then straightened them, as though to relax tension.

"This is a very old system. Must be at least twenty years old, but it's still adequate."

"I'm so surprised," I said, fingering the thick records. "Mr. Loop told me they were electronic chimes and I thought somehow real bells were played electronically."

He laughed, the same indulgent chuckle I had heard when Dickie said something cute.

"No," he said, "we select the records we want it to play. These are pretty old, because we've learned the old songs touch the hearts of most people. See," he picked up the top record, "here's the 'Old Rugged Cross.' When people hear that, especially those who were brought up in church, it reminds them of their childhood faith."

He moved toward a clock-like instrument. "Come here, Louise. I think I'll teach you how to set the timer and change the records in case I should be out of town or something." He looked at me and smiled faintly. "Or so you can teach a new pastor."

I knew he was kidding, but I remembered what Shirley had said last night. The thought that he might not be called again in October distressed me, and I had an impulse to talk to him, and tell him everything the people were saying. I wanted to let him know I intended to help. But if I told him anything, I would get Roy into trouble.

"I hope I never have to teach a new pastor," I said sincerely.

"Well, you never can tell," he said, and bent over the timing mechanism. I looked at him, at his wide shoulders and thick neck. A shiver went through me as I thought—*what if he had caused his wife to commit suicide?* I could scarcely concentrate on what he was telling me. My hands shook as he had me put a record in place.

"It'll be good," he went on, "for you to come up with the repairman and let him demonstrate it again."

"But I won't usually be changing the timer, will I? I mean, why would the thing have to be changed?"

"Only when daylight saving time starts, or when we change in the spring," he explained. "But, yes, I'd like you to consider this one of your jobs. You can make your own record selection—you know, we can't have the same hymns playing for weeks at a time. Buy some new ones if you want."

I drew in my breath apprehensively.

"I hope I do it right."

"How could you do it wrong?"

I glanced at him and stifled an impulse to laugh as I thought how terrible it would be if somehow I got the records mixed up and put on rock and roll.

Richard was gone when the repairman came, but before he left he gave me a duplicate key. When I opened the door to the tower, the repairman said, "Oh, a dead bolt. You don't see locks like this very often."

"Really? I don't know a dead bolt from a live one." He smiled slightly at my attempt at humor.

"No, there aren't many like this around anymore. But with so much vandalism going on, the police are recommending this kind of a lock. With these, you have to use a key. They can't be opened with a credit card like the others."

Upstairs, he looked at the equipment and whistled. "Man, this stuff has whiskers on it. I doubt if I have parts for it." He opened his tool kit and began to paw through it for parts. I watched him for a moment or two, then said, "Do you need me? I have some letters I want to get in the mail."

"Naw. If I can find the trouble, it probably won't take me long."

"Okay," I sighed, relieved. "I'll be in my office." I turned to start downstairs. "Oh, there is one thing—the pastor wanted you to demonstrate it to me before you leave."

"Fine. I'll come get you when I'm ready."

I had just started transcribing when Roy peeked in my office. The sight of him always made me feel as though I were plunging down in an elevator.

"Hi, Miss America," he said softly. He came toward my desk, then looked out the window.

"Whose truck?" he asked. I explained about the chimes and his eyes twinkled with amusement.

"Have you had any complaints from the neighbors yet?" he asked.

"No, but I wouldn't be surprised. You can't imagine how loud those chimes sound at three o'clock in the morning."

"I'll bet," he grinned and jingled some coins in his pocket as he walked around the room. I couldn't help but watch him. He was attractive in a new white shirt, and there was a faint spicy scent in the room. I wondered what kind of shaving lotion he used.

I had to fight myself to keep from daydreaming my favorite dream where I would just be leaving my office and he would be coming in. We would collide, and then he would take me in his arms and kiss me.

I actually felt dizzy now as I looked at him. In the back of my mind I knew I would have to hurry to get the letters transcribed and in the morning mail, but at the same time, I hoped Roy would never leave. I tried to think of something that would detain him, but my mind wouldn't come up with anything.

He came close to my desk and saw the little dark key. He picked it up and looked at it carefully.

"What's this? Oh, I know. The bell tower. I have one, too." He took out his leather key case and picked out its twin. "See?" He put the key back on my desk.

"The pastor gave it to me this morning," I volunteered. "He wants me to make the record selection from now on." I smiled up at him, "Part of my job."

"You mean you have to climb those rickety old stairs every so often? Watch out, or the bogeyman will get you."

"Ooh! Quit it, Roy!" I cried. "It's spooky enough up there. Maybe not spooky, but it makes me feel smothered. I hate to be in close places." I shuddered. "I even hate elevators."

Roy smiled sympathetically. "Claustrophobia?"

I nodded.

"Poor baby!" he said, mocking. "Well, I've got to get to work."

"Wait a minute, Roy." I held up my hand. "I want to tell you something important." I had suddenly remembered my dinner with Shirley the night before.

"Anything you have to say is important," he spoke flirtatiously and then became serious. "But say it fast." He twirled his finger to speed me up.

"I had dinner with Shirley last night and she told me the same thing you did."

"About what?"

"About the money and the pastor. You know."

His pleasant manner changed to wariness. His eyes narrowed and his hands became quiet inside his pockets. He stared at me, waiting for me to go on.

"I told Shirley I didn't believe the pastor would do anything so stupid." My tone was almost defiant.

"Stupid?"

"Yes, stupid. To take money from a safe for which only he and Mr. Loop have a key is stupid."

"Of course it is, but he undoubtedly thought he could put it back before it was missed. Or maybe he thought he could change the cash slips or something.

"That's just it, Roy. He is too intelligent not to figure it all out and make it foolproof before he did it. Besides, there's no need. He isn't rich, but he makes a good salary."

"There's never enough money, though," Roy said, shaking his head. "Louise, I wouldn't try too hard to look for reasons, if I were you. He took the money. Of that I'm sure."

"I still think he's innocent," I said. My chin lifted. Although I was in love with Roy, I could not agree with his attitude toward Richard. "And I'm going to try to prove it."

"Do you think Gerald did it?" Roy had a sarcastic look on his face.

"Gerald?"

"Gerald Loop."

"Oh, no. You said he wasn't even here. Besides, he hasn't any reason to steal a hundred dollars, either." I bit my lip and frowned. "I don't know who did it, Roy. I'm going to keep my eyes and ears open, though, and try to find out."

I rested my elbow on the typewriter and put my chin in my hand. "Maybe somebody wants to make Richard look bad."

Roy shook his head and smiled sweetly. "More power to you, Louise. It's refreshing to see someone who is loyal to her employer." His unblinking, sapphire-blue eyes looked straight into mine.

I could feel myself blushing again. He made me feel like a high school girl cheering for the football team. I breathed deeply and squared my shoulders. He started to leave.

"Roy, one more thing—"

"Yes?" he seemed pleased for me to detain him.

"Where is the safe? You know, the one—"

He rushed back to my desk and pinched my cheek.

"Oh, you poor little darling. So many things in this big world you don't know!" He held out his arm to me. "Come along. I'll show you."

I smiled and stood up, but I didn't put my arm through his. I didn't trust myself. Instead, I stepped behind him.

"Lead on!" I made a sweeping, you-first gesture.

He led me down the hall beside the sanctuary and across the narthex. Our feet made no sound on the carpet, but Roy kept up a constant monologue about how deprived I was that I had never been on a first-class tour of the church property.

"You see, my dear, just to the right of the main entrance is a closed door." Again he took out his key case and produced a shiny key. "But—voila! I open zee door! And there you see a miniscule, but complete office, where ushers' carnations and offering plates are stored, tithes counted, and underneath this carpet," he pulled back a three-by-five oriental rug, "is the safe in question."

I looked at the round brass plate cover on the safe, which was set in cement, flush with the floor.

"How clever!" I exclaimed. "A thief would probably never think to look under a rug. And it surely would be impossible to open that without a key."

"Now you are beginning to understand," Roy said and looked at me with bright eyes.

I felt my mouth tighten as I nodded my head in agreement.

Roy straightened the rug, we backed out of the tiny office, and I watched him close the door.

On the way back to our offices, we walked past the open door that led to the tower room. We both glanced up the stairway.

"I guess the repairman is still up there," I remarked.

"He'll probably recommend a whole new system," Roy said. "That would be the most logical thing, anyway."

"The pastor said the system was still adequate."

Roy flashed a look at me, but said nothing.

In my office, I saw that the mailman had already come. I was provoked with myself for letting the morning get away without doing my work. Roy must have felt the same way because, as he looked at his watch, he said. "Do you realize, young lady, I am having to come to work earlier now that you're here? I can't seem to get my work done during the day for running in here to talk to you."

I gazed into his eyes and felt myself lean toward him. I was so happy I could hardly keep from touching him! He cared for me.

At that moment, Vanessa Hamilton knocked on the door-facing.

"Hello," she said in her cultured voice. "Am I interrupting anything?"

"Not a thing, my dear Mrs. Hamilton!" Roy bowed and turned to me. "Miss Bridges, I trust you won't have any more trouble with the chimes." He eyed Vanessa appreciatively. "I hate to leave you lovely ladies, but I must." He turned and gave me a special look, then walked briskly from the room.

"What did he say about the chimes?" Vanessa asked, but her eyes were on the closed study door.

I gave her a brief account, then said, "Pastor isn't in, but I think he'll be back late this afternoon."

"Oh, too bad," she pouted. "A friend of mine has just opened a Mexican restaurant a few blocks from here and I thought it would be a good way to show our Christian interest by going there for lunch." *Vanessa, the things you cook up,* I thought.

Her shoulders drooped and I noticed tiny lines at the corners of her mouth. She looked at me with dull eyes.

"Louise, how about you? Do you like Mexican food? Go to lunch with me."

I was startled. Eating lunch with Vanessa was the last thing I wanted to do. And yet, the thought of a beef enchilada with melting cheese was enticing. I looked at my watch.

"It's only eleven-thirty," I said, "and besides, the repairman is still working up in the tower."

"No, I'm not," the stocky, smiling repairman said as he

came into the room with a clipboard in his hand. "It's done, and it works perfect. Should last another twenty years!" He laughed loudly as he held out the clipboard for me to sign.

I clapped a hand over my mouth. "Oh! I was going to have you demonstrate it, remember?"

The repairman's mouth drooped and he looked at his watch. "Oh, yeah. Well—"

"Never mind," I smiled at him. "You go on. I'm sure I can put the records in place. If I have trouble, I'll call you."

"Right!" He grinned, snapped the clipboard shut, and left.

"So. Do you want to go to lunch with me?" Vanessa asked.

"Thank you. I love Mexican food." But I had an odd feeling in the pit of my stomach. I was sure I felt exactly like a fighter just before he enters the ring.

I had never ridden in a Cadillac. The interior was a blue brocade material. It made a perfect setting for Vanessa. She looked like an advertisement in an expensive magazine as she placed her lovely hands on the wheel.

With easy, relaxed motions, she maneuvered the big car through noonday traffic. In five minutes or less, we pulled into an almost vacant parking lot behind a small, newly-painted building. A big sign featuring a cactus plant and a sombrero read, "Dos Amigos." It was a hot day, but Vanessa was unwrinkled and beautiful as she led the way through a dark, ornate door into a small waiting room.

A buxom Mexican woman hurried toward us, clapping her hands and smiling warmly. Her eyes were large, almost round, and her eyebrows were heavy and black. Her shiny black hair was piled high in an intricate arrangement of curls.

"Vanessa!" she said loudly, and extended her arms. "You came to eat good Mexican food?" There was a slight trace of Mexican accent.

"Hi, Lisa, dear," Vanessa said, presenting her cheek for a kiss. "I promised, didn't I?"

"Come! I want you to sit where everybody outside can see you!" She smiled at me and led the way to a window booth. She gave us menus and hurried to get ice water.

"I knew her in high school," Vanessa explained. "And then later her husband worked for mine. Now they're going to try this.''

She looked around at the small dining room, and I got the impression Vanessa wouldn't be eating here again. "I hope at least, she's a good cook.''

The food was good—much better than our stilted conversation. We talked a little about the weather and the school, and I tried to tell her about a Scripture that had especially thrilled me, but there wasn't much response. I felt I was walking uphill in lead shoes.

She asked me a few polite questions about my work and social life, but there were long silences, and I looked forward to the time when the meal would be over.

I was sure Vanessa felt the same way. She had only asked me to lunch because Richard wasn't available, and because she had wanted to keep her promise to Lisa. Her questions to me weren't because of a genuine interest. I hated superficial conversation. I wished I could break through her facade and know her better. Maybe I could even like her if I understood her feelings.

For one thing, what was her opinion of Richard? I knew she was attracted to him, and probably in love with him, but what did she think of him as her pastor? I savored the last bite of the delicious enchilada, then took a big gulp of iced tea.

"Vanessa," I began timidly, "have you heard anything—unkind—about the pastor?''

Her eyes widened and she quit chewing.

"What do you mean, unkind?''

"Well," I compressed my lips and played with the iced tea spoon. "Some are claiming he stole a hundred dollars from the safe.''

She sucked in her breath.

"That's ridiculous!" Her eyes narrowed and I couldn't tell from her expression if she had heard the accusation before.

I nodded my head.

"They're also saying they may not call him next year.''

Vanessa looked down at her plate, picked up a ripe olive and chewed it thoughtfully. At last she said, "It might be better if they didn't call him. He might be happier if he were forced to go someplace else.''

66

She blotted her lips carefully and looked out the window. "It might be nice to be someplace where there were not so many memories." Her eyes, for a moment, were large and wistful.

I looked at her carefully, trying to read her mind. She didn't want the pastor to leave, did she? Wasn't she in love with him?

"But it would be terrible to leave under a cloud of suspicion, wouldn't it?" I asked.

She closed her eyes and shook her head in a superior way I hated. "Don't worry. Richard's not the kind to run from trouble."

Her eyes narrowed suddenly. "And what do you think of the story?"

"I agree with you; it's ridiculous. He's too intelligent, too genuine to steal. And I intend to help clear him." As soon as I said it, I realized how childish and boastful my remark sounded. She became very still and looked at me critically. I began to blush.

"What I mean is, I'm going to try—to try to get to the bottom of it." She continued to stare at me and I began to bite my lower lip. I tipped up the empty iced tea glass and a big piece of ice fell down on my mouth.

"Well, Louise," she said with a cynical smile, "I'd tread softly, if I were you. Remember, you're dealing with older and wiser people than you—Christians. I wouldn't rush around accusing, if I were you. You just might possibly find yourself in a strange city without a job." She underscored her statement with an icy look that lasted for several seconds.

I batted my eyes hard as I felt hot tears pressing against them. I shrugged my shoulders and fumbled in my purse for compact and lipstick. At last, I recovered enough to speak.

"I've got to get back, Vanessa. I didn't get my work done this morning."

"Yes," she said briskly. "I have some dittos to run off for W.M.S. this afternoon." She picked up the check, and left a tip.

We rode almost in silence back to the church. I couldn't think of anything to say that wouldn't be insulting. I did thank her for lunch when I got out of the car, but I hurried to my office, without waiting to walk with her.

At my desk I made myself turn off the part of my mind that wanted to repeat her remark. Or was it a threat? Anyway, I had to forget it and get my work done.

About 2:30, I finished my transcription. Then I remembered that the chimes had to be reset. I picked up the little key and walked quickly down the hall past the sanctuary and stood before the tower door.

I unlocked the old-fashioned bolt and skipped up the narrow stairs two at a time. It was hot and stifling up there; I could smell roof tar and old, hot wood.

I examined the record player and tried to remember everything Richard had told me. I went through the old records, selected three and put them in position. At that moment, I heard a click. It was not a click in any of the equipment. The click was in the lock at the foot of the stairs.

8

I stood motionless beside the record player and held my breath. Maybe I had imagined it—I hoped. There was no sound now. No movement, no breath of air. Suddenly, I felt smothered and I filled my lungs with hot, stale air. I crept over to the stairwell and listened.

The louvers high above me spotlighted millions of dust particles in a thin ray of sunshine. The particles floated silently in the hot air. Perspiration made my hair cling to my neck and cheeks as I leaned over and peered down the stairs. With lead feet, I moved silently down the stairs, one step at a time and, as I knew it would be when I got to the bottom, the door was closed. I had left it open. I fell against it and frantically twisted the doorknob, but I was locked in.

"Oh, God," I whimpered, "help me!"

I beat on the door with a clenched fist and shouted, "Help!" I kicked until my toes hurt. For a moment or two, I completely lost all reason, I was so terrified. I couldn't stand it. I could not bear to be locked in.

I raced back up the stairs and jumped up on one of the dusty benches with the hope of calling out through the tower louvers, but they were too high. Aware of my own moaning and sobbing, I clasped my hands and squeezed with all my might in an effort to calm down.

"Oh, Father, help me, help me. Make someone find me!"

My heart was thudding through my body and my mouth was dry as I ran down the stairs again. I would pound and yell until someone heard me. Richard would be back sometime this afternoon. He would miss me, if not at the office, then at dinner time. I felt a little calmer.

When I got to the bottom step, I saw the edge of a piece of paper under the door. Had it been there a moment ago? I didn't know. I began to shake from the center of my stomach on out through my legs and arms. I stooped down and picked it up and sat down weakly on the steps. It was just a small scrap of paper, perhaps torn from a desk pad, and folded once.

On it was a childishly drawn cat, lying on its back with all four legs sticking straight up. The cat's face was in profile, and instead of an eye there was a plus sign. Underneath the cat was one word, "CURIOSITY."

It didn't take a genius to get the message. "Curiosity killed the cat," and I was the cat. But why? I folded the paper into a tiny square and tucked it in my shoe.

My mind darted over recent conversations, first with Shirley then with Roy, and just a couple of hours ago, with Vanessa. Shirley wouldn't hurt me, would she? I knew she didn't like the pastor very much, and I had declared my intention to support him and to try to solve the mystery about the stolen money. But I had gotten the impression last night at her house that she would be glad to see his name cleared.

"It would be wonderful if somehow it turned out that he is innocent," Shirley had said.

Surely not Roy? He had shown me in so many ways he liked me. Perhaps more than like. He wouldn't be this cruel to me. But, I remembered, we had talked about claustrophobia not long ago. Maybe he locked me in for a prank? "NO!" my heart cried.

Vanessa. She had practically threatened me. And I knew she

didn't like me. But it didn't make sense. Why should she care if I tried to find out the truth? If she really cared for Richard, and I believed she did, wouldn't she be glad for him to be completely exonerated?

But there was something cruel about Vanessa. Everything about her seemed cold—at least to me. She had probably locked me in to scare me. I had left the key in the lock on the outside, and all she had to do was close the door and turn the key.

The realization that I was locked in washed over me like a giant wave. I leaped up and began to scream and pound on the door again. Exhausted, I leaned against the wall and gasped for breath. Everything was quiet. No response—just thick, suffocating silence.

The timer! I could reset it so it would start playing *now*. And when the thing began to play the tinny sounding hymn at this time of day, someone would realize there was something wrong. I would be saved!

I raced up the stairway, two steps at a time, past the landings, and stood panting beside the mechanism. In moments, the tower was vibrating and clanging, "Abide With Me."

When Harry Van Buren unlocked the door, I almost threw my arms around him.

"Why, Miss Bridges! What on earth are you doin' here?" he asked, his small eyes open as wide as they would go. The hot space was filled with his odor and I pushed by him quickly. I was close to tears, but I was laughing, too.

"Somehow I got locked in," I said. I wondered if I should tell him that someone had locked me in. But, in that moment, I knew it would be better to pretend it was an accident.

"Locked in? Oh, no!" Harry Van Buren frowned and smiled at the same time. "When I first heard the chimes I was cleanin' over in Fellowship Hall, and I thought to myself that the pastor or Mr. Decker would take care of it," he smiled and shook his head, "but after about three minutes, I finally decided maybe I'd better do something."

"I wondered why it took so long," I said. "I knew the pastor was gone, but I thought Roy—Mr. Decker—would come and let me out."

"Well, how could you get locked in? Because—"

"Did you find my key in the door?" I countered.

"There wasn't no key in the door." He held up his enormous key ring. "I opened the door with my own key."

"I just don't know how it happened," I answered truthfully. "I had gone up to set the timer after the repairman worked on it, and when I tried to get out, I couldn't."

"Isn't that the limit!" He shook his head again and said, "Well, you're okay now, so I'd better get back to work."

"Oh! Stay here just a moment, will you, Mr. Van Buren, while I go back up and set the timer again, please?" I didn't give him a chance to answer, but ran up the stairs, set the mechanism and raced back down.

"Thanks for waiting," I said, out of breath. "I really appreciate it."

"That's all right." He smiled warmly. "Guess Esther and me just have another child to take care of!"

"Oh, you!" I smiled and stamped my foot. I resisted the urge to defend myself and tell him about the threatening note. Some inner caution made me decide to keep the whole incident to myself.

"Mr. Van Buren," I called as he started down the hall, "please, please don't tell anyone I got locked in the tower. "It's so—" I groped for the right words, "it makes me look so stupid."

"Mum's the word!" He put a big, dirt-creased index finger to his mouth.

"And will you please lock this door? I can't imagine what happened to my key."

He ambled back and locked the door, then shuffled away. After he was out of sight, I bent over and looked at the carpet near the door, but I couldn't find the key. Evidently, whoever had locked me in took it with him—or her.

I was so hot and disheveled from being in the tower room, I decided to go home and take a shower. I went to the office to pick up my handbag and the first thing I saw was a little dark key, right in the center of my desk. I started to pick it up, then hesitated. Would it have fingerprints on it? Maybe I could have it dusted, or whatever police did. But, I decided, that was sort of melodramatic. I couldn't do that by myself and I wasn't going to tell anyone my suspicions about Vanessa. I would just go along, pretending that everything was the same. But I would keep my eyes open and, sooner or later, she would reveal her guilt.

I had just opened the drawer to get my purse when the study door opened. It startled me because I hadn't expected Richard to come back until later. He stood in the doorway with a strange expression on his face. I couldn't tell if he looked flustered or irritated, but he didn't seem especially friendly.

"Where have you been?" he asked. His voice was courteous, but his eyes were hard. "I tried to call the office about noon, and then again at one, and finally decided I'd better check to see if anything was wrong."

"I'm sorry," I said, suddenly conscious of how messy I must look, "but, first of all, Vanessa came by to ask you to lunch." I watched his face to see what reaction he would have, but there was no change.

"And since you weren't here, she insisted I go with her to this new Mexican place some friend of hers has opened."

He looked at his watch meaningfully.

"I wasn't out to lunch all this time. I got locked in the tower room." I had blurted out the truth without thinking.

"Locked in the tower room? How?"

"I really don't know." I bit my lip. I was so mad at myself. I hadn't intended to tell anyone. "How long have you been back? Didn't you hear the chimes?"

"I can't imagine how you could get locked in," he said, ignoring my question.

"Maybe there was a gust of wind or something. Like a ninny, I left the key on the outside instead of taking it upstairs with me."

"But there isn't any way you could be locked in," Richard said, his features changing from coldness to concern. "Accidentally, I mean. The key would have to be turned."

"Well, that's what I thought, but somehow I got locked in and Mr. Van Buren came to my rescue. I finally remembered I could set the chimes to go off, and he heard them. Didn't you hear them? It was just a few minutes ago.'' He looked beyond me then and I turned and saw Roy standing in the other door.

"Oh, hi, pastor," he said. "I just came to tell Louise the repairman evidently hadn't fixed the chimes. They went off a few minutes ago, and, of course, it was a good excuse for all the students to get out of hand."

He laughed, but his eyes flicked back and forth and his hand played with the stapler on my desk. He always seemed ill at ease with Richard.

"It's just a matter of re-setting, I believe," the pastor said, before I could explain. "We'd better get back to work."

After Roy left I said, "I've already reset the timer. I'm sure it will go off when it's supposed to."

"Well, let's go up and make sure," Richard said. I followed him down the hall toward the narthex. "And, Louise, it isn't necessary to tell anyone you got locked in the tower room."

I looked up at him and frowned. He turned and saw the question in my eyes. "It just seems peculiar, and I would rather you didn't mention it for now."

For the fourth time that day—not counting the times I ran back and forth like a trapped animal—I climbed the tower stairs. This time I preceded Richard and wondered self-consciously if he was looking at my legs. Up in the room, Richard examined the mechanism and nodded his head.

"You've got it set right. Good girl." He turned and looked at me and ran his fingers inside his collar. "It is HOT up here. You poor girl. Were you scared?" He smiled slightly and his eyes had a strange expression in them.

"I was terrified!" I started down the stairs, hurrying as I remembered how horrible it had been to be locked up. I ran down the narrow staircase and out into the cool narthex. Richard was right behind me and, after he locked the little door and put away his key, he brushed his hands together, as though he had accomplished a dusty, disagreeable task.

As we walked along the hall toward the study, he walked slightly behind me. I looked back at him. "Do you have any special work for me this afternoon?"

"No, not really," he answered. "When I was trying to reach you earlier, I wanted you to look up some statistics, but I've already done it."

"I'm sorry," I said. "I'll be glad to do anything you want—"

"No, no," he said. "Why don't you go home and try to relax? I'm sure this has been a hard afternoon for you." His words were tender, but his face was stony, expressionless.

"I'd be glad to have a shower," I admitted. I would be glad to get away from him and the church tower.

In my own bright, little bedroom, after a long cooling shower, I felt much better. But there were still many unanswered questions. Who would be so cruel as to lock me in the bell tower room?

I didn't like Vanessa, but after thinking about it for awhile, I couldn't believe she would do such a childish thing. Childish—maybe that was the answer. Maybe one of the school children had been sent into the church for something, saw the key in the door and decided to lock me in, just out of orneriness. I would be sure to ask each of the teachers if any of their students had been sent on errands or had been missing for awhile.

But that wouldn't explain the drawing of the cat. I unfolded it and looked at it. It might have been drawn by a child, but what child knew about my decision to find out the truth about Richard? Besides, Roy had told me the children were never allowed in the church except by special permission.

As for Roy—he had been involved with school business at the time. At least he implied that he had been. He said the students had used the bells as an excuse to get out of hand.

Shirley couldn't be considered. Her thirty pupils kept her busy every moment of the day. I put the drawing in my jewelry box and thought about Richard.

When had he returned? He had been in the study when I first came down from the tower room. Had he been in the building during the time I was locked in? How long had he been in his study? Long enough to get some statistics. But wait a moment—he didn't know anything about my resolution to clear his name, and even if he had, there would be no reason to threaten me. I was his ally.

Ally! What a strange word to be used in a Christian organization. But I knew, as certainly as I knew where to put my fingers on typewriter keys, that something was terribly wrong here at Arboleda Heights Christian Church and School.

There was a knock at my door and, as I called, "Come in," I pulled my robe sash tighter about my waist. Dickie came in holding a big photograph album.

"Would you like to see pictures of my mom and dad and me?" He smiled up at me shyly.

"Sure I would!" I patted the bed. "Here, sit beside me." He climbed up and opened the book between us.

"My mom put all these pictures in, and the first one is her as a baby and then a little girl, and then my dad when he was a baby, and then a little boy, and then—"

"Why don't you just start showing them to me?" I hugged his thin little shoulders.

"Oh! I almost forgot." He pulled a folded square of paper from his pocket. "I made this for you."

I unfolded it and saw a peculiar drawing, carefully colored, of some kind of vehicle.

"Thank you, Dickie. Is it your wagon?"

He looked up at me indignantly. "It's a *funny* car!"

"Oh, of course! Thank you. You colored it nicely." There was a similarity in the drawing to the one tucked in my jewelry box.

"Dickie, can you draw cats?"

"Of course," he said and flipped his hands up. "But I'd rather draw racers or dinosaurs."

I gave him a sidelong glance. Had he drawn the cat? More important—had he locked me in?

9

It took about half an hour to listen to Dickie explain every picture in the album. After we had looked at the last picture and closed the book, I realized I had learned a lot about Pastor and Mrs. Fitzsimmons.

One thing was as clear as a new pair of glasses. They had been a happy couple. I saw that Pastor Richard could be hilarious and even a little idiotic on some occasions, as I remembered one snapshot of him standing on his head with eyes crossed. He was certainly a different man in the family album than the somber man I worked for.

There had been a couple of pictures of him in a football suit, and one in a baseball uniform. He had been tremendously handsome in both. There were many pictures of him as a loving father, some holding Dickie as a baby, or pushing him in a swing or walking up a pathway holding his hand.

With a husband like that, why would Vera want to commit suicide? It didn't seem reasonable, and yet, that had been the verdict. She had been smiling in most of the pictures and seemed to be a happy, healthy mother and wife. Of course, most people smile when they are having a picture taken.

Dickie got off my bed and went to look at the things on my dresser.

"This was my mom's dresser," he said. "She had pretty bottles like yours, too."

"You had a lot of fun with your mom, didn't you?"

"Yeah." His thin little fingers touched one of the perfume bottles. "This summer we were going to Knott's Berry Farm and to Disneyland." He hunched his shoulders slightly.

"I'm sure your dad will take you." It was hard to keep from hugging him, he seemed so pitiful. But he could also be hateful and perhaps vindictive.

"Maybe he'll take me," Dickie said, "but I doubt it. He doesn't do anything fun anymore!"

I clapped my hands and drew in my breath.

"Maybe *I* can take you! I've always wanted to go back to Disneyland."

In the mirror I could see his eyes widen with pleasure. Then he turned, leaped up and fell on the bed.

"Ya-a-ay!"

"Now calm down, Dickie. I said maybe. We'll have to get permission, and figure out a way to go—I don't have a car—and we have to wait until school is out." He was clapping his hands in quick little pats, nodding yes.

"Right now you go get washed up for dinner."

After he left my room, I laid back across the bed. It was

76

still hot and the upstairs room was stifling. I held up the drawing of the funny car Dickie had given me, and the whole episode in the tower room came back to mind. I had always hated enclosed places. There had been times I felt panic inside a car with all the windows rolled up. There would be future times when I would have to go up to the tower room to change records or reset the timer. The thought caused my heart to beat in rapid, heavy thuds. I just couldn't go back up there unless someone was with me.

Dickie was playing with the water in the bathroom, turning it on and off in pipe-rattling jerks. Could he have been mean enough to make the cat drawing and then lock me in? I jumped up quickly, took the drawing out of my jewelry box and compared it to the funny car. They were similar, yet who but an expert could tell if the same person had made both of them?

I stood before the open window, but there wasn't a touch of breeze. The hot sun beat down on the asphalt parking lot and shimmering heat waves rose from its surface. If it was this hot today, what would it be like in the middle of the summer?

For the last two weeks there had been a growing restlessness at school. There was only a short time now until school would be out. Almost every day there was something special going on—Hot-Dog Day, May Festival, or Student Bake Sale.

As each day unfolded, the children seemed harder to control. Shirley, Beverly and Roy had all threatened to quit—kiddingly, of course—and Harry grumbled quite a bit about the extra cleaning he had to do.

During this time, I became better acquainted with school parents and church members, and could honestly say I loved my job. Richard was a professional in his work and I admired him more each day.

Gerald Loop came in several times a week to pick up the extra funds that were gleaned from the various activities. He seemed always to be in a good humor, but there were a couple of times I caught him looking at me, and his eyes were calculating, almost hard.

My giddy heart flip-flops continued when I was with Roy, and although he still did not commit himself, I was convinced he cared for me. There were a few things about him, however, that I couldn't understand. For one thing, his preoccupation with money bothered me.

"This church and school has a ridiculous budget," he complained one day. "How can we do a decent job on pennies?" Another time he said, "I should have stayed in radio, or gone on television. I'd make a lot more."

Another thing that upset me was his continual chipping away, indirectly of course, at Richard. He would ask, "How long has it been since we took in new members?" Or, "Did you notice how empty the church seemed Sunday?" Or, "I heard a good man preach on TV last night. What a challenge it is to hear preaching like that!"

I knew he didn't like the pastor and it was apparent that Richard didn't care for Roy either, although he never said or did anything against him. It was what he didn't do that let me know how he felt. He never smiled in welcome when Roy had to see him on school business. They never went to lunch together, and the pastor never invited him to the parsonage for a meal. There was no love between these brothers. When I remembered the Bible verse, "Behold how they love one another," I felt sad.

One eighty-five degree day, just before school was out for the summer, I had gone home to shower and put on a light robe. I was on my bed reading when I heard footsteps on the stairs, then a soft tapping at my door.

"Yes?" I said, jumping off the bed and straightening my robe.

"It's Richard." I heard him clear his throat. "May I talk to you?"

I glanced at myself in the mirror and pulled my robe sash a little tighter. My long hair looked almost white as it swung loosely around my shoulders. When I opened the door, Richard's eyes widened slightly.

"Come in," I said.

"I'm sorry—I didn't know you weren't dressed." His chin lifted slightly and his eyes seemed cold.

"It's so hot," I explained.

"I would like to talk to you, but I'll wait—" he started to turn away.

"I'll dress and come right down."

As Richard went downstairs, I turned to the closet. It was so hot I couldn't bear the thought of anything tight. I chose a shift in a Hawaiian print of blue hybiscus which seemed to make my eyes bluer. I put on a little lipstick, a dab of perfume on each wrist, then ran downstairs.

Richard was waiting for me in his chair. He rose to his feet and smiled slightly. He was in shirt sleeves and had taken off his tie. I caught a faint aroma of shaving lotion and I was aware of his masculinity. He motioned toward the couch and I sat down.

"Louise, the more I think about it," he said as he sat back down in his chair, "the more concerned I am about that day you were locked in."

He gazed at me until I looked down. "By the way, you smell nice." He said this in the same tone he might have said, "You type well."

His remark was out of character and, although I was pleased, it caused me to fight for composure. Finally, I said, "Well, I'm certainly concerned about it. I was scared to death."

"I know you were. Frankly, the incident scared me, too."

I looked up at him and his dark eyes were luminous.

"I haven't told anyone my suspicions, but now that this has happened to you, I've decided to confide in you. Somehow I believe this tower thing has a direct connection."

I swallowed and felt a shiver of fear run through me. "Connection? To what?"

"I think someone, or maybe a group, has decided to try to get me to resign."

I caught my breath, but I wasn't really surprised. Shirley had said she didn't think he would be called in October. If there were very many against him, it would be better if he did resign.

"And I don't want to resign," he continued, as though reading my mind. "Even though Vera's gone, this work is my life."

He stopped talking and stood up. He peered around the divider to see if Esther was in the dining area. When he was convinced we were alone, he went on.

"Don't misunderstand me. If the Lord wants me to move on, I'll move. But I don't want to be forced away from His work, if it isn't His will."

He looked down at the carpet through clasped hands and I could see the muscles in his jaw contract.

"So far, the Lord has always put the desire in my heart first, when it's time to move. But I'm almost certain there's an evil force at work—something that will destroy the work if it isn't stopped."

He looked at me and his wide-open eyes reminded me of Dickie. I had an almost overpowering impulse to go to him, reach out to him. And yet, I wasn't sure of this man, in spite of what I had said about believing in him. Someone had locked me in that tower, and it could have been Richard.

"Louise, has anyone said anything to you about me?" I thought of the things Roy, Beverly and Shirley had said about him. I had been brought up to believe evasion was as bad as lying, but I didn't want to get any of my co-worker friends in trouble—especially not Roy.

I sat on the couch, dumb, and felt the color creep up my neck and into my cheeks.

Richard's chin lifted and his nostrils flared. "I can see you've heard some gossip."

He stood up and looked out the front window. His back was to me and I could see that his shirt was damp across his shoulders. He rattled the change in his pocket and his right leg twitched impatiently. He turned suddenly and faced me. The look of anguish in his eyes touched my heart.

"Louise, please help me!" he whispered. "Please tell me what they're saying so I can fight this thing."

I felt as though I was being pulled apart. Surely, surely Richard was all he claimed to be. But, how about Roy? Wasn't he a good man, an honest man? What should I do? Roy had insisted I forget what he told me about Richard. Could I betray him now by telling the pastor of Roy's accusations?

Without thinking it through, I said, "I'll tell you what I know, with one provision. Please don't ask for names." He gave me a hard look, then sat down.

"They're saying you must have driven your wife to suicide."

His eyes narrowed with sudden hatred and a deep frown brought his heavy brows together. His chin jutted out, his mouth drew down, and his whole face and attitude frightened me. He looked capable of anything.

"And?" His voice was a growl.

"They say you stole that money out of the safe."

He closed his eyes for a moment. His face looked grey. He was beginning to need a shave and he looked old. I tried to compare this man before me with the laughing football player in Dickie's photo album. Could they be the same man? Was my decision to help him the right one? Or would it drag me down too?

But when he opened his eyes and looked into mine, I knew I would help him, whatever way I could.

"And—" I continued, "you were right about someone trying to get you to resign. They *are* saying you won't be called again in October."

He sighed heavily. I longed to touch him, to comfort him.

"Esther and Harry?" he asked. "Do they feel—do they want me to leave, too?"

"Oh, no! Well, I don't know about Harry. I never have a reason to talk to him, but I know Esther loves you like a son. I'm sure Harry does, too. And they feel like grandparents to Dickie."

Suddenly, Harry was standing there in the living room. I wondered how long he had been there and if he had heard any of our conversation. But he had a smile on his face, although his eyebrows gave him a slightly worried look.

"Esther ain't feelin' very good tonight, Pastor. She was wondering if Louise here could get you folks your supper? I have to go on an errand this evening and I thought I'd pick up a hamburger on the way. Esther says she don't know if it's the heat or what, but she's got a bad headache and don't want nothin' to eat."

I jumped to my feet, concerned for Esther. "Of course I can fix dinner. But first I think I'll go see if Esther needs anything."

Harry put up his hand gently to stop me.

"I'm sure she don't," he said. "In fact, she might've

dropped off to sleep now."

"Oh, well," I said, "then I won't disturb her."

"She'll be okay, come mornin'," Harry said. "Once in a while she gets these bad headaches, but they never last more'n a day." He smiled at us. "I'm leavin' now, but I'll be back 'round nine, I'm sure." He turned back toward the kitchen.

After he closed the back door, Richard "whewed" out his breath, shook his head and smiled. Neither one of us said anything about Harry's odor, but we both saw the joke in it and grinned widely. Suddenly, it was a light and happy moment between us and I felt close to him.

"Well!" I said, and tossed my hair back over my shoulders. "I guess I better get in the kitchen and see what I can fix."

"Have you been down to the beach recently?" Richard asked.

"I've never been to the beach here in Los Angeles."

"Are you serious?"

"Yes! Shirley and I keep saying we'll go some weekend, but it either turns cold and overcast, or she has to work."

"We'll go this evening," he said authoritatively. "I know a place that serves good seafood, and it's right on the ocean. We'll get Dickie, and if we hurry, we can see the sun set."

Dickie was ecstatic at the prospect of seeing the ocean. He ran across the playground and back to us twice before we reached the huge building at the back of the property which comprised the garage, storerooms and Fellowship Hall.

Although I had attended a couple of carry-in dinners in Fellowship Hall, I had never had a reason to go into the garage. An ordinary door faced the playground and I knew there were three large garage doors in the back that opened out onto the alley. I had seen them several times when Shirley took me shopping. She always brought me home through the alley and let me off at the back of the playground because it was closer to her apartment. The playground was always well-lighted and I had never been afraid to cross it, even after dark.

Although it was still daylight when Richard put his key in the garage door, I felt a shiver of fear as we entered the gloomy, three-car garage. Richard didn't always put his Ambassador station wagon away, especially if he had called on someone late in the evening. On those occasions, he parked in the front lot, but today when he had come home, I suppose he thought he was through for the day because he had put his car in the garage.

The space assigned to Harry and Esther was empty, but huddled over against the wall was the late Mrs. Fitzsimmons' Volkswagon.

Richard opened the overhead garage door and the afternoon sunlight revealed a heavy coat of dust on the VW's emerald green finish. I felt dreadful as I looked at the little car, knowing she had died in it. I wondered if she had struggled before she died? What if she had changed her mind at the last? I shuddered and made myself look out at the sunlit alley beyond.

Richard seemed to be unaware of the little car. He opened the door of the station wagon for me and I let Dickie in first so he could sit in the middle. I glanced again at Vera's car. The gruesome thought occurred to me: a coffin on wheels. Why didn't Richard get rid of it? After we had driven out of the alley and started toward Arroyo Drive, for the second time that day he answered my unspoken question.

"I guess I should sell Vera's car. I could use the money." He turned west and the sun almost blinded us.

"I wondered why you kept it," I said. "Doesn't the sight of it depress you?" Dickie looked up at me and then at his father. His eyes were round and sad.

"Strangely enough, it doesn't," Richard said. "It somehow—" He seemed to grope for words. "It—has comforted me."

We drove for awhile without talking, then he added, "Vera's dad gave her the car shortly before he died. He wanted to do something special for her. She had told him how tied down she was because I had to have the car all the time, so he bought it for her. He smiled, remembering.

"He even paid for the license, because he knew I couldn't." He glanced at me self-consciously.

"Sometimes Mom let me guide," Dickie said. "Not on busy streets, but sometimes she let me turn in the alley."

"She did!" Richard seemed surprised. "I didn't know about that."

"And she taught me how to shift gears, too. She used to

put her hand over mine on the gear shift knob. I know how!"

He doubled up his fist and pushed it toward the panel. "That's first! Bar-r-oo-OOOM!" He yanked his fist back toward his leg. "And there's second—Bar-r-oo-OOOM!" "And, there's—

"Okay, okay son," Richard interrupted, patting Dickie's leg. "We believe you." Dickie kept up an undertone engine sound as he pretended to drive.

"Anyway," Richard continued, "Vera's car was like a part of her. She was so active in the work, calling on sick folks and on her Sunday School pupils, and picking up people Sunday morning. I just can't bring myself to get rid of it."

I thought I understood, at least a little. I had packed everything Leslie had ever given me in a cardboard box and asked my Aunt to keep it for me.

"But I'm going to have to do something about it," he said. "It hasn't been out of the garage since—that day." He looked down at Dickie who was driving his own car in fantasy land.

After a few moments, Richard looked over at me.

"Do you think it was my fault? I mean about Vera?"

"No," I answered truthfully. "That was something I didn't get a chance to tell you in the living room. I don't believe any of those things they say. And I told Shirley that—" I caught my breath as I realized I had mentioned her name. But he knew how often we were together. He had probably surmised Shirley was one of the "they."

"What was it you told Shirley?"

"I told her I believed in you and was determined to help clear your name."

"Thank you, Louise," he said quietly. "Have you told anyone else?"

"That I wanted to clear your name? Why?"

"Because, as I told you earlier, I think your experience in the tower has something to do with me."

"I think so, too."

"So, if there's anyone else—but, of course, I promised not to ask for names."

"I told Roy, Beverly, and Mrs. Hamilton," I blurted.

"Vanessa? Why did you tell her?"

I blushed as I remembered our conversation. I had started it and, in a way, it had been gossiping. But this was no time to be evasive.

"I asked her if she knew what people were saying about you—and I told her I intended to get to the bottom of it."

"Vanessa believes in me."

It was a statement and I looked at him quickly to see if I could read his thoughts. His face was expressionless as he maneuvered through evening traffic.

"Yes," I agreed. "But she did say perhaps you'd be happier if you went away and got a fresh start."

"She has told me the same thing."

We were on the Santa Monica Freeway now, and the sun was hard to face. I looked at him through squinted eyes. His face had a golden look, but he was also squinting, concentrating on the traffic.

"Maybe we shouldn't have come," I said.

"Why?" He glanced at me quickly. "You mean the traffic? It'll thin out. Besides, the dinner will be worth it."

I relaxed a little, but there was a sadness in the car. I sighed as I imagined how much fun this could be if Richard was Roy—or, if I was Vera.

After awhile, Richard turned off the air conditioner and opened his window.

"I want you to smell the ocean." His brown eyes twinkled. "Dickie always likes to smell it."

"Yeah!" Dickie exclaimed and sniffed deeply.

I inhaled, too, and the damp, salty smell excited me. Dickie and I both sat up straighter and began to look for the ocean. We came up over a hill and, suddenly, there it was. Dark and light blues, greens and gold—the Pacific Ocean. A rippled path of gold led to the sun, resting on the horizon. I caught my breath. How could anything be so beautiful?

In minutes, we had parked near a rambling white building trimmed in blue. Beside the front walk there was the weathered hull of an old boat in the yard, and there were heavy ropes and life preservers leading to the door. Richard opened it and Dickie rushed in. As the hostess smiled at us, I became aware of the hot pressure of Richard's hand on my back.

10

I was shocked to think Richard would touch me, but I was even more startled at my reaction. My heart began to beat faster and I felt the color come up in my cheeks. What was the matter with me? I felt thrilled and yet ashamed.

I knew now I had gotten over Lester. Our love, though a sweet memory, was just that—a memory. For weeks now, Roy had filled most of my idle thoughts, but at this moment the spot on my back where Richard had touched me seemed to be on fire.

What kind of a person are you, Louise? Are you so starved for love you react like an animal? I hated these thoughts. I lifted my chin and stiffened my back as I walked primly behind the hostess to our table.

Richard seemed almost jovial as he studied the menu.

"What will you have, Louise?" he asked. His former gloom and concern seemed to be completely gone. "Have anything you like. You, too, Dickie—and don't say a hamburger and a malt." He winked at me. "How about scallops, buddy? Remember? You liked them."

"Mmm! Yeah," Dickie said and patted his stomach. "I'll have scallops."

"Louise, what will it be?" He looked boyish now, much like his football picture. "Get lobster if you want."

The prices were unbelievable, which made me remember the stolen money. Had he taken it? He had said he ought to sell the VW so he could have the money. I looked up at him and was embarrassed to see how tenderly he was looking at me.

"I'll have shrimp," I said and immediately regretted it. What was the matter with me? I didn't really like shrimp. I just wasn't functioning properly. I was going to have to get a firm grip on my emotions before I made a real fool of myself.

"Cocktails?" a waitress said, her hand poised over a pad. I watched Richard's eyes to see what his reaction would be to her short, revealing sailor suit, but he scarcely looked at her.

"No, thanks," he smiled and looked at her face. "We would like our coffee now, though, please."

We were seated at a window facing the ocean. We could hear the rhythm of the waves because the ocean came up under the building.

"Dickie, look," I said. "We can pretend we're on a ship." He looked down at the water slapping the dark pillars and grinned.

"Can I be the captain?"

"Aye, aye, sir," I said. Dickie laughed out loud, then turned to Richard.

"How do captains get the boat to start?"

"I'm not absolutely positive, but I think the captain tells the chief it's time to go, and he moves an instrument that let's the engineer know what the captain said." Richard winked at me again, and his answer seemed to satisfy Dickie.

"I think I'd rather be the engineer," he said, and then began a quiet pantomime of shifting gears and steering. As I looked at Dickie, I realized I was beginning to be attached to him. In some ways he seemed a little spoiled, but most of the time he was loving and obedient. I hadn't seen him have a tantrum since that first time in the office.

"I couldn't take my lizards with me on the ship," he said gravely.

"Why not?" I said. "You could keep them in your cabin if you were the captain." He smiled then and I wondered what he was thinking. I still wasn't used to those reptiles. I sincerely wished they *were* on some ship in the middle of the ocean.

"The sun is almost down," Richard said. The ocean had turned a reddish purple and the sky was watermelon pink with rays of gold.

"It's beautiful!" I tried to fix the scene in my memory. I looked at Richard. The sun made his eyes glow. He turned to look at me and I had a strange sensation inside.

"You look like a twelve year old girl," Richard said.

"I'm not a girl," I said primly. "I'm twenty-three years old." He continued to look at me searchingly. "Nine years younger than I." He sighed, and I felt my heart begin to pound heavily. It was a relief when the waitress brought our salads. For the rest of the meal, our conversation was either on Dickie or affairs of the church.

Once during dinner, he stretched his long legs out and brushed mine. We both sat up quickly and I tucked my legs under my chair. I had known Richard only three months, and at first I hadn't even liked him, but gradually I had learned to admire him and then, finally, to give him my loyalty. But deep in my heart I still wondered if he had *borrowed* the money.

Now, tonight, I was aware of him as a man. A tall, strong, mature man. Roy seemed far away. I felt compelled to stare at Richard.

He was explaining something about having a quorum at business meetings, but I didn't know what he had said because I was watching his face. It must be this restaurant, I decided, or the sunset. That was it. I hadn't had much fun for a long time, and my emotions just didn't know how to handle an evening like this.

"You haven't heard much of what I've said," he accused.

"No, I haven't." I giggled and looked down at my lap. We finished our meal quietly, but occasionally we looked at each other, then away.

When we were finished, he said, "Let's go home, kids." He stood up and put some bills on the table. Dickie and I walked out to the parking lot while Richard paid the check. It was cold now, and I wished I had brought a sweater. Dickie suddenly threw his arms around my waist and I could feel him shivering. When Richard let us in the car, Dickie snuggled up to me and it seemed natural for me to put my arm around him.

"How can it be so hot in the daytime and freezing at night?" I asked.

"I'll turn the heater on in a minute," Richard promised. On the way home, Dickie fell asleep, and his towhead slipped lower and lower until it was in my lap.

Occasionally, Richard glanced at me, but we said little on the way home. I didn't trust myself to say anything. I was accusing myself of being fickle and giddy and many strange thoughts were thrashing around in my mind.

As we turned in the alley behind Fellowship Hall, I thought I saw a light go out in the storeroom.

"I wonder if Harry is back," I said.

"Why?"

"I saw a light in the storeroom go out just now."

"Are you sure? I didn't see it."

"I'm sure I did."

"Maybe it was just the reflection of the headlights when we turned in the alley." I shrugged, but I had gotten an impression of a light being turned out in the corner window where the storeroom was.

I woke Dickie while Richard opened the garage door. The headlights picked up the shape of Vera's car, but the space where the Van Burens kept their camper was still empty.

"See?" Richard said, when he drove the station wagon into place. "Harry's not back yet. It must have been a reflection on the window."

"I guess so," I said. Outside, I looked up at Esther's and Harry's apartment. "No light on up there, either. Hope Esther is all right."

"She'll be fine in the morning," Richard said in a hushed voice.

Dickie stumbled a few times as we crossed the playground but, by the time we were in the house, he was wide awake.

"Can we watch television, Dad?"

"I thought you were ready for bed." Richard looked at me. "Shouldn't he be in bed?"

"It's only eight-thirty," I said.

"Well, buddy, if there's anything worth seeing, you can stay up for half an hour."

When we got inside, Richard turned on the lights and switched on the television. Dickie got the TV Guide and brought it to his father.

"Let's see, now," Richard said as he opened the little magazine. The sight of him in his chair, Dickie leaning against him, filled me with a strange yearning.

"What do you want to see, Louise?" He looked up at me and his eyes were soft.

I couldn't stay in this room! I couldn't trust myself. I had to be alone—to try to sort out my emotions.

"I'm tired," I said and covered my mouth as though stifling

a yawn. "I think I'll go on up and read awhile, then go to sleep."

Richard seemed disappointed and I was tempted to stay—but I waved at them and went up the stairs.

In my room, I went to the mirror and looked at myself. I seemed to be a stranger. Had I fallen in love again? The thought filled me with both pleasure and contempt. I compressed my lips and frowned.

"Louise, Louise!" I whispered to my image. "You don't know what kind of a man Richard is. Don't forget Vera!"

I looked around my room. She had lived here, dressed, read, looked in this mirror, and she and Richard had slept in that bed. What had driven her to end it? Now, more than ever, I felt determined to dig for the answers.

I took another shower and tried to quit thinking of Richard. I tried to think of Roy instead, but couldn't seem to bring his face to mind.

A cool—almost cold—breeze was coming in the window when I got into bed and it felt good to get under the blanket. I propped up my pillows and picked up my Bible. It fell open to the 119th Psalm and I began to read:

"Thy word is a lamp unto my feet, and a light unto my path." What a comfort! He will guide me and help me get the facts. A light unto my path—light! *Had* I seen a light in the storeroom or not?

I sat straight up in bed. There was no way for me to see Fellowship Hall from my room, but I had to know what I had seen. I got up, put on a dark blue slack suit and tennis shoes. I knew Richard would never let me go back to the garage alone. He had sounded determined when he told me it was probably a reflection from the car's lights. I would have to wait until Richard and Dickie went to bed.

In a little while, I heard Dickie say, "Good night, Dad. See you in the morning."

I turned out my light and closed the door which led to the bathroom as he began to clump up the stairs. I didn't want Dickie to come in and talk to me tonight. I waited in the dark a long time, then quietly opened my door.

It was dark downstairs and I hoped Richard was in his room

with the door closed. I glided downstairs and out the front door. I was especially careful to leave it unlocked so I could get back in.

The light from the parking lot made it easy for me to see how to open the wrought iron gate and I crept noiselessly along the side of the parsonage. I waited for a moment at the back door and looked across the huge, silent playground. There was a light on in the storeroom! The window was on the far side of the building, but I could see a pale yellow oblong of light on the pavement.

I couldn't risk running diagonally across the playground, so I hurried along the chain link fence that bordered the property until I reached Fellowship Hall. I walked cautiously toward the lighted window and, as I came within earshot, I heard Harry say, "This here's a Polaroid, ain't it?"

"Yes, but it won't bring much. Obsolete." The man's voice was low, scarcely more than a stage whisper, and I couldn't recognize it.

I leaned forward to peek in the window. I saw Harry's face, but the other man's back was to the window. They were squatted down; their attention was on a peculiar assortment on the floor. I saw a cassette tape recorder, several suitcases, some cases that were probably film projectors, and record players.

I was in a painful position and took a step to one side to relieve my back. There must have been a small hole in the pavement, because I turned my ankle and lost my balance. The movement made a scuffing noise; I ducked below the window and held my breath.

"What was that?" I heard Harry say.

"Probably a cat," the other man whispered. "Good grief, Harry, why don't you have those blinds shut?" I heard the metal slats clack together, and I could no longer see in the storeroom.

What were they doing? Did that equipment belong to the church or the school? I knew it must be about 10:15—pretty late to be sorting or cleaning out the storeroom. When did Harry get back anyway?

I stepped around to the alley and saw his camper. There was some light and I could see that the back door was open. I tiptoed over to it and looked in. I couldn't see too well, but I made out a television set—a big one—and beyond it, there was a grandfather clock on its side on top of the camper cushions.

"Let's get the rest of this stuff unloaded," I heard Harry say. I barely had time to scoot to the front end and duck down beside the hood before the two men came out of the garage door.

"My wife was sick tonight when I left her," Harry went on, "and I didn't know we had to go to two places."

The other man didn't answer, but I could hear them both grunt and whisper as they moved the TV into the storeroom.

As soon as they were out of sight, I ran around the building and straight across the playground. Each breath I took was like a hot knife in my chest. I didn't know what they were doing, but I knew whatever it was it must be wrong, and I would be in plenty of trouble if they caught me spying on them.

I opened the gate, then the front door, and dashed up the stairs into my room. I gasped for breath and my heart felt as though it would jump out of my body. What was Harry up to? And who was the other man?

I had sat down on the bed and started to untie my tennis shoes when I decided to back downstairs and wake Richard. He would know what those men were doing and whether or not it was wrong. There was probably a reasonable explanation, but I wanted Richard to know about it.

I had started down the stairs when I remembered my determination to unravel the mystery of the money taken from the safe. Could it be that Harry had stolen the money? I knew he carried a big ring of keys, and, although Shirley said no one but the pastor and Mr. Loop had keys to the safe, it *could* be possible for Harry to have one. He had all the freedom in the world to be in any part of the church or school. What would keep him from hiring a locksmith to have one made?

I went back to my room and closed the door softly. I had to think. Why had I run away awhile ago? If I had kept my head, I might have learned something by now. Suddenly I knew I had to go back to the Fellowship Hall. If I was going to solve anything, I would first have to find out what Harry and that man were doing. I was sure there was a connection.

I was becoming an expert at creeping up and down stairs, opening doors and gates without making noise. The thought almost made me giggle. I ran silently across the playground toward the corner of the building. There was no light from the window now, but I could still hear their muffled voices. I moved close so I could eavesdrop. I was aware of the sound behind me, but it was too late. The blow on my head sent me sprawling forward, and my face hit the pavement.

11

In the comic strips, there are always stars when one of the characters gets a blow on the head, and I discovered it is true. When I was hit that night, a flash bulb seemed to explode in my head; then, I had the impression of blue stars. That's all I can remember about my "accident." Accident—that's what Richard and Harry said it was.

"Pastor, all's I know is," I heard Harry say as I regained consciousness, "I had put the camper away and was comin' around the building when I found Miss Louise, stretched out on the pavement."

I was on the couch in the living room and Richard was seated beside me, holding a wet washcloth on my head.

"She must have tripped in a chuckhole or something," he added.

"A strange accident," Richard said softly. "I don't see how she could have hit the top of her head." He turned the cloth over and I shivered at its coldness. "She would have had to turn a somersault to raise a knot like this."

I opened my eyes and looked at Richard and Harry.

"Why, hello there, Miss Louise," Harry said tenderly.

Everything I had seen out there in the storeroom surged into my mind. Was Harry actually going to pretend he didn't know anything about it? I started to sit up, but Richard held me down.

"Be still," he said. "You may have a concussion. I've called Doctor Fowler."

Again, I tried to sit up.

"I'm all right, Richard, but I have to—"

"Shush—wait until Doc has looked at you. Then you can talk." He kept one firm hand on my shoulder and held the washcloth on my head with the other.

I relaxed briefly, but as I realized what had happened, a slow, cold fear again took possession of me. Also, I was beginning to feel nauseated.

There was a staccato knock at the front door and Harry lumbered over to open it.

"By George, Pastor," Dr. Fowler groaned, "Louise is the only person in the church I'd be willing to come out in the middle of the night to see."

Richard stood up to make room for the doctor. It was comforting to have him beside me. He was one of the older church members, and, for some reason, we had been friends from the start. He had a good sense of humor, and I didn't feel shy with him, as I did most people. He taught an adult Sunday School class, and the whole church seemed to love him. Maybe I would have an opportunity to tell him what I saw out there.

"Let's see, now." He tipped the shade of the lamp so the light flooded the top of my head. His gentle fingers touched the bump and I winced. He parted my hair tenderly, and pursed his lips, "Hmmm."

He took my pulse and temperature, then said, "You'll be okay." He winked at me. "Be surprised what these old skulls can stand. And, you're not bleeding—no broken bones, either!" He laughed and shook his finger at me.

"I'd be ashamed if I were you! Running around on the playground at your age!"

He dabbed some medicine—which stung like fire—on my face, then stood up. He picked up his neat little bag and was out the front door before there was a chance to say anything to him.

Richard hurried out after him and they talked for a few moments. Harry came and stood over me and, for an instant,

I'm sure my eyes reflected the fear inside. But his face was as kind as a St. Bernard's.

"I'm sure sorry about your accident. Esther'll have a fit when she finds out you were out there in the dark."

He looked at me as though waiting for me to volunteer the reason, but I couldn't speak.

Richard closed the front door, and Harry lifted his arm in a good night wave.

"I'd better git on upstairs," he said.

After he was gone, Richard fanned the air and gulped as though choking, shook his head and blew out a short breath. I smiled, then realized an important fact. Harry *couldn't* have been the one who struck me. I *know* if it had been Harry who raised his arm for the blow, I would have *smelled* him.

After awhile, Richard allowed me to sit up and, for an instant, I thought I would throw up. I leaned back against the couch and closed my eyes again. Richard sat down beside me and began to smooth the hair back from my forehead.

"What were you doing out there, Louise?" His voice was soft.

I opened my eyes and looked at his face, only a few inches away. "You know when we came home I told you I thought I saw a light in the storeroom?"

"Yes, I remember."

"Well, it bothered me. And I knew you would say no if I told you I wanted to investigate."

"So—you took matters in your own hands, fell down in the dark and just about fractured your skull—you dopey little character."

I smiled up at him, then my eyes dropped down to his throat. His collar was open and I could see a little tuft of dark hair just above the top button of his shirt. I had a strong desire to lean over, put my head on his chest and let him hold me.

Then—it came to me that he had on the same shirt and slacks he'd worn to dinner. My mind flashed back to the night he had come out of his room to have cocoa with Dickie and me. That night, he had worn his bathrobe.

I calculated from the time I heard him tell Dickie good-night, and added the time I had waited in my room.

He certainly should have been in bed when Harry carried me in—but, here he was, fully dressed. Why? Hadn't he gone to bed? Why not?

"And what did you find out, Miss Curious? Were the lights on?"

I felt cautious. Maybe he already knew the lights were on. He might have been out there himself. Well, whatever, I didn't want to lie.

"Yes, the lights were on."

"So—did you see anyone in the storeroom?" Again, I hesitated. I was conscious of how cold my hands were as I rubbed them together. Couldn't I honestly say I didn't know for sure? I really didn't know who the other man had been, and, at this stage of the nightmare, I didn't want to tell on Harry.

"The blinds were shut," I said. "Richard, I'm sorry I've caused so much trouble," I turned my face away. I knew now that someone didn't want me to find out his—or her—secrets, and I was also convinced that, when I did learn the truth, I would discover who took the money out of the safe and why Vera had committed suicide.

If only there was someone I could trust—someone who would help me put the puzzle together! If only I could really know and trust Richard. Sometimes I felt close to him. For a little while this evening, I had even imagined I was in love with him—but, right now, I was a little bit afraid of him.

"I think I'd like to go to bed," I said.

"I'll help you." He stood up quickly.

The stairway was almost too narrow for us to go up side by side, but he held me in a firm grip until we were inside my room.

"I'm fine now," I said. "Thank you."

"I'm not going to leave you until you're safely in bed."

"But I'm not ready for bed," I protested.

"I'll wait," he said, and stepped out into the hall. "Call me when you're in bed."

Self-consciously I got out of my clothes and into my gown, brushed my teeth and washed my face—tenderly. I was going to have an ugly place on my cheek for awhile.

After I came out of the bathroom and started to get in bed

I noticed it—a scrap of paper on the floor beside my tennis shoes. My head ached when I bent over to pick it up.

A dead cat was scrawled on the paper. I felt a knot form in my stomach. My hand began to shake as I looked at the ugly cartoon. How had it gotten in here? Richard? Of course not! He wouldn't be so childish and melodramatic. But how did it get here? Obviously, it had been tucked in my clothes by whoever had hit me.

"Louise? Are you all right?" Richard called in a stage whisper.

I wadded up the scrap of paper and stuffed it in my jewelry box along with the other one, then got into bed.

"Yes, I'm in bed."

"I want to see for myself." He opened the door wide enough to see me. I held the sheet tightly under my chin.

"All right," he said. "Now, you stay there. I'm going down the hall to check on Dickie." He started to close the door, then came over to the bed. He had such a stern look on his face I had a moment of terror. What was he going to do? He reached down to the foot of the bed, pulled the blanket up and tucked it around me.

"Even though it was hot today, it's cold now." He snapped out the lamp. "Good night, Louise."

Later, I heard him coming back from Dickie's room, and then heard his footsteps as he went down the stairs.

I don't know if I slept very much or not. It seemed to me I was awake most of the night. Finally, when it was just beginning to get light, I gave up trying to go to sleep, put on my bathrobe and tiptoed downstairs to make coffee.

I half hoped Richard would come into the kitchen for his breakfast, and I lingered over two cups of coffee and a piece of toast. I saw by the kitchen clock that it was time for me to get ready for work, so I rinsed out my cup and saucer, looked once again at Richard's closed door and went upstairs. I wondered if Esther would be able to get up this morning. If not, I would fix Dickie's breakfast, but first I would get dressed.

I was combing my hair, carefully avoiding the bump on my head, when I heard Esther's voice downstairs. I was glad she was better. She was like an aunt to me, and though her constant talk was sometimes tiring, I loved her.

Did she know anything about Harry's activities last night?

Even though it had seemed strange—Harry in the storeroom so late, moving furniture from his camper and talking to a stranger—there might be a logical explanation. I was tempted to ask Esther, but if she didn't know anything about it, she might be upset. I didn't want to do anything that might make her sick again.

When I went downstairs, I walked over to her and kissed her on the cheek. She looked pale and older this morning.

"I'm so sorry you were sick yesterday," I said.

"Oh, I'll be a'right, honey. I think the heat kinda got to me, but when I went to bed yesterday afternoon I sure went sound asleep. I don't b'lieve I woke up once until about four o'clock this mornin'. 'Course, I had in my earplugs 'cause Harry snores. That sleep did me a world a good." I nodded my head and gave her a hug.

"I've got to go, Esther. I'll be late." I hurried out the door. She didn't notice my bruised cheek and obviously she didn't know anything about last night. I wasn't going to be the one to tell her—at least, not right now.

When I got to my office, I could hear Richard's voice, loud and authoritative. Though his door was closed, I could hear every word.

"The Bible says, 'a house divided against itself cannot stand.'"

"So, are you telling me that I can't have an opinion?" This was Roy, also loud and angry.

"Of course not! I'm saying if you have definite opinions or valid suggestions, come to me first. Don't undermine the work."

"Undermine the work!" There was a tense silence. I stood motionless at my desk, afraid to open the drawer to put my purse away. I had never heard them quarrel before, and I was embarrassed and a little frightened. I didn't want them to know I was eavesdropping.

"If anyone has hurt the work around here—" Roy's voice stopped in mid-sentence, loaded with unspoken meaning. There was another long silence; then Richard spoke, lower this time and I couldn't understand all his words.

"—not argue. But—not tolerate—insubordination."

"Thank you, Pastor! Thank you for letting me know my place!"

I realized the "conference" was almost over, so I grabbed my purse, ran down the hall and into Beverly's office.

As usual, her hair was beautifully done and her makeup was flawless. As I came up to her desk, I was aware of her lovely, expensive fragrance.

"Hi, sweetie," she said and continued to sort and file papers. "I thought I saw you sail by my office awhile ago."

"You did—"

Beverly paused in her work and looked up at me.

"What's wrong?"

"Roy and the pastor are having words."

"I'm not surprised. Roy has been griped for days. Hey! What's wrong with your face?"

I reached up and touched the skinned place on my cheek.

"Oh, like a dummy, I fell last night. It's not serious. What were you saying about Roy?"

"He's getting more and more irritated with the pastor. He wants him to resign."

"Oh, I know," I said. "I wish he didn't feel that way about him."

"Still think he's the Great White Father?" She lifted an eyebrow and smiled.

"I think he's great!" The words burst out emphatically. Beverly shook her head.

"Honey, I know how you feel, but let's face facts. He's simply not the lily-white man of God you want him to be."

I turned away and studied the mimeograph machine. I ran my finger across the top of it, turned my hand over and looked at the smudge of ink on my fingers, then turned back to her.

"Beverly, do you honestly—down deep in your heart—believe that Richard—" I realized I had used his first name and began to blush— "the pastor took that hundred dollars?"

She straightened a pile of papers, picked up a pencil and tapped it lightly on the desk. Over her coy, half-lenses she said,

"Louise, when I first joined this church I thought Pastor Richard was the next thing to God. He was a wonderful preacher and pastor." She smiled wistfully. "I remember he came to see me every day a few years ago when I had my operation." She made a few marks on a scratch pad.

"And I thought the world of Vera, too. We were on lots of committees together and we were close." She put the pencil down and clasped her hands as though in prayer. "If I ever had a problem. I could tell either Richard or Vera and I *knew* they prayed for me."

"Well, why have you turned on him then?"

"Lots of reasons, honey—lots."

I felt a surge of anger. I wanted to stamp my foot or shake her arm, but instead I said calmly, "What things? Well, besides that money?"

She spread her hands out on the desk. "Okay. Number one—when Roy first came about three years ago, Richard said he needed an associate. And it was evident from the beginning, that Roy loved to preach—and Louise, he is *good*. Well, at first the pastor let him preach about every four to six weeks, but when he realized the people enjoyed him so much, he quit letting Roy take his turn at the pulpit."

I frowned. It was hard to believe Richard would be jealous."

"Oh, Beverly, are you sure that's the reason he isn't allowed to preach?"

"What other reason?"

"I don't know, but—"

"How long have you been here now, three months?"

"Just about—but Beverly, maybe Roy's messages weren't as Scriptural—"

"I'll have to admit his messages aren't expository, and maybe they're a little flamboyant," Beverly said, "but they get to your heart. He's a real charmer."

"I know," I said—and wished I hadn't because Beverly looked up at me and I began to blush.

"All right, back to why I've changed my opinion—to sum it up, I've discovered that our pastor has feet of clay, that he's jealous of Roy."

"But Beverly, do you know this for sure? I mean, maybe

he has asked Roy to speak and, for some reason or other, he couldn't. How do you know Roy hasn't been invited to speak?''

"Because Roy has told me—lots of times. Poor man. When he came here he thought he would be sharing equally in the pastoral duties and responsibilities.''

"But isn't being principal of the school just about all he can handle?''

"Yes, and that brings me to the second thing. Pastor Richard has continually blocked all Roy's efforts to get help at school. Roy really needs an assistant himself.''

"Mr. Loop told me that you run the school.'' I smiled at her.

"Ha!'' She sniffed, but I could see the remark pleased her. "Well, I do work hard. But I don't have to meet with irate parents or discontented teachers. Roy's job is a hard one, and he's underpaid too, but the pastor is so conservative he keeps the raises small and far apart.'' She wrinkled her nose.

"I could get a lot more for this kind of work in a public school.'' She was quiet for a moment or two. "But back to Roy—Richard won't even let Roy run the school the way he wants to. For instance, Roy would like to introduce new techniques. He'd like to experiment with some of the ideas the public schools are using. He wanted to take out all the desks in fifth grade, and let the children sit on mats, or bring their sleeping bags to class so they would experience a freedom in their work. But the pastor absolutely vetoed it. He almost had a stroke when Roy was telling him his plan.''

"To tell the truth, Beverly, I can't imagine a classroom like that, either.''

"Why not?'' she challenged. "Times are changing. Children have television and Disneyland and everything under the sun to amuse them. School shouldn't have to be a drag.''

"What did the pastor say?''

"Just a big NO! He said people sent their children to Christian schools to get away from crazy ideas like that. He said a lot more—but the thing I wanted you to see is that he won't let Roy share in the ministry and he won't let him run the school.'' She stood up and went to the coffee pot that was always plugged in.

"Coffee?" She poured some in her little china cup with roses on it, then poured mine in a styrofoam cup. It tasted horrible.

"And then, when Vera took her own life—" Beverly shook her head. "That really did something to me. I just can't help but blame the pastor."

"He really seemed to love her," I offered.

"Yes, I think he did. But something must have happened. Something so terrible—something that hurt her so much—that she couldn't take it."

Beverly looked at me pointedly. I thought of Vanessa. Could they be having an affair? I quickly rejected the thought. It made me almost physically sick.

"And then, the hundred dollars was stolen, and all of us on the inside know that the pastor never seems to have enough cash."

"I wonder why? The financial report shows he makes a good salary. A hundred dollars! What good would it do to steal a hundred dollars?"

"I don't know. But Dickie has been sick a lot, and the church doesn't provide health insurance—although I don't think Doc Fowler ever charges him as much as other people."

She looked at me sharply. "Don't quote me, Louise, because I don't really know what he charges." She drank some of her coffee, leaned back in her chair and ran her finger around the edge of her dainty cup.

"And, of course, the pastor's mother is in a rest home back east. That's a tremendous drain on his income."

"I guess!" I murmured.

"He has to have decent clothes—being in the pulpit every Sunday—and a reliable car. The church does buy his gas."

Just then Roy bounced into the office and his face was bright and smiling. If I hadn't heard part of the argument, I would never guess that he'd been angry only moments before.

"What have I done to deserve to have my two favorite women waiting for me?" He spoke with arms outstretched.

I looked at him, his face tanned, his eyes brilliant with humor, immaculately groomed, and my heart quickened.

What had possessed me last night to think I was in love with that somber, sad-eyed preacher? This was the man who attracted me. Someday, I was sure, he would invite me on a real date. Maybe to as nice a restaurant as I was in last night with Richard.

"Louise, are you waiting to see me?" he asked. Our eyes locked for a heart-dropping moment.

"Yes and no," I laughed and my voice sounded high-pitched. "Did the pastor tell you about the accident I had on the playground last night?"

Beverly looked up quizzically.

"Accident? What accident?" she asked. "You told me you fell down."

"What happened?" Roy asked, suddenly serious.

"I thought I saw a light in the storeroom last night," I began. There was no point in protecting Harry, I decided. If he was doing something wrong, then he should be exposed.

"In the storeroom?" Roy interrupted. "Can you see it from your room?"

I had to think for a moment. For some reason, I didn't want to tell them I'd been out to dinner with Richard and Dickie. Now I'd probably have to tell them, because under normal circumstances, I would never have noticed a light out there.

"I didn't exactly see a light in the storeroom, but just sort of a glow on the pavement." I looked at both of them and felt guilty. "Anyway, I didn't want to bother the pastor, and Esther was sick last night—"

"She was?" Beverly asked. "What was wrong with her?"

"The heat, I think. Maybe a migraine. She's fine this morning. Well, anyway, I ran out the back door and across the playground and was almost to the window when I—" I couldn't say I had been hit on the head, at least not yet, "—when I sort of tripped and fell."

"What a little dopey!" Beverly "tsked" at me.

"—and somehow I bumped the top of my head."

"That's a shame," Roy said and looked at me strangely. Then he turned to Beverly. "Excuse me for changing the subject but Bev, have you pulled the file on that little Montoya girl? Her mom's coming in this morning."

"Oh! That's right!" Beverly wheeled around to the file. "I've got some up-dating to do."

"Louise, come into my office," Roy said. "I'd like to hear the rest of this."

I realized Roy had skillfully manipulated the conversation so I could spend a few moments alone with him. I was elated.

I followed him into his office and heard the soft click of the door. I looked at him expectantly, trembling inwardly. But his manner was businesslike. He sat on the edge of his desk and motioned toward a chair.

"When you got out to the window last night, did you see anyone?"

I almost said, "Harry," but then I thought of Esther. If I told Roy I had seen Harry and some other man, he might want to make it public. When I thought about it I realized that what Harry was doing wasn't really any of my business and it could hurt Esther if I talked about it. Also, I had no desire to get hit on the head again, so I said, "No, I couldn't see because the blinds were down."

If I ever told anyone whom I had seen, I would probably tell Richard, but right now I was disappointed. Why was Roy asking questions about last night? Wouldn't he ever be romantic? Wouldn't he ever tell me that he cared?

"If you didn't see anyone, did you hear anyone talking?"

I shook my head, and felt guilty again.

"Maybe you just *thought* a light was on out there."

"No! I know there was a light—it might have been Harry, because he's the one who found me on the playground. He'd been somewhere and had just come home—he said."

I felt my left eyebrow raise a little. Why didn't I just tell Roy everything I knew? I had to trust somebody. But as I looked at him, staring at me without a trace of a smile, there was an inner caution, some restraint that told me I could trust no one. Someone had struck me on the head, hard enough to knock me out, and that meant someone didn't like me.

The thought not only frightened me, but it hurt my ego. I had always been shy, easygoing, never one to assert myself. Why or how had I gotten myself into a situation where I was not only disliked but definitely not wanted?

"How did you say you got that place on your cheek?" Roy asked, reaching out and gently touching the abrasion.

"When I fell," I said. "Richard said he couldn't understand how I could skin my cheek and hit the top of my head, too." I looked at Roy, hoping he would see I needed protection.

"Did you say you turned your ankle?"

"I don't know what happened, really. Harry said I must have stepped in a chuck hole."

Roy chewed on the inside of his cheek and nodded slightly.

"That's probably it. Stepped in a hole, fell forward on your face, then sort of bounced back on your head."

We suddenly laughed at the idea of me bouncing around in the dark.

"Well, whatever it was, it sure hurt," I said. I stood up. It was time for me to be at work.

Roy stood and took a step toward me. He looked deep into my eyes and I felt a thrill in my stomach, as though I was dropping, dropping in an elevator.

He put both his hands on my shoulders, gently, and I was conscious of how large and warm his hands were. My heart began to beat crazily, and I closed my eyes. *He's going to kiss me.* His hands moved up slowly until they were on my neck, and the pressure was firm, almost uncomfortable. I opened my eyes. His lips were only inches from mine when he spoke.

"Don't go out in the dark, anymore." His voice was soft, almost a whisper. "You might really get hurt." He pressed a little harder on my neck, then released me. His hands slid to my shoulders and he gave me a little push.

"You'd better leave while I'm able to let you go." He turned his back abruptly and walked around his desk and sat down.

I felt completely frustrated. I thought I loved this man. I had daydreamed for weeks of the time when he would be this close to me. But there was something about his embrace that frightened me. I flipped my hair back and smoothed it, took a deep breath and turned to leave.

"I'll see you later," I said over my shoulder with a carelessness I didn't feel.

Roy's huge, blue eyes commanded my attention. "Remember," he said, "no more sleuthing." I smiled and left his office.

Bev was busy at her desk and scarcely looked up as I hurried by.

"Have a nice day," she called absently.

I touched my throat as I walked down the hall toward the study. I should be happy. Roy had finally shown me that he cared. But a premonition that something dreadful was about to happen poked holes in my joy bucket. For an instant, I almost wished I could go back to Portland.

12

A week passed. I had put my accident out of my mind as much as possible as I helped Beverly, Shirley, and the other teachers the last few days of school.

The children were wild and required constant discipline. There were lots of special things scheduled: WIENIE-BANANA DAY, when the kids could buy hot dogs and chocolate-coated bananas; COSTUME DAY, much like Halloween, except all the costumes were supposed to be patriotic. Even the teachers dressed up that day, and regular classes were practically suspended. Then there was DECATHLON DAY—a word I had never heard—which meant a sports day, full of races and athletic events, with blue ribbons, lots of shouting, music and loudspeaker instructions.

During these days, Richard excused me from my desk as often as I was needed by the school, and every day was filled with excitement and fun.

On WIENIE-BANANA DAY, I served hot dogs to at least fifty kids. Another day, Shirley and I almost got hysterical laughing at one another in our Betsy Ross and Martha Washington outfits.

On DECATHLON DAY, I stood in the smoggy sun and cheered runners who were doing their sweaty best. I helped teachers keep their students from tearing down crepe paper streamers, putting banana peels on the walk, or grabbing white wigs off would-be George Washingtons. I loved it, and through it all, like a heartbeat, was my infatuation with Roy.

I watched him constantly. He ran with the kids and strutted in his Uncle Sam costume. The children loved him, and I did, too. But I was more shy and reserved with him since that day in his office.

I didn't see much of Richard that week. He had to go out on church business every night and didn't return until I was in my room. Dickie and I were drawn closer through the school activities and our evenings together. I had even gotten brave enough to hold his lizards and, to my surprise, I actually thought they were kind of cute.

Harry lumbered back and forth, unusually good-natured, considering all the extra cleaning he had to do that last week. Esther went about her regular housework and, though she seemed a little wan, she talked as much as ever.

At last school was out and the place was almost unbearably quiet. Beverly came in every morning about nine and worked until noon, and Roy was in his office a part of every day. I don't know exactly what he did, but he seemed to be hard at work whenever I saw him. But there had been some subtle change in his attitude toward me. I didn't understand it, and it disturbed me.

Shirley went to her mother's place in San Diego for the summer and I missed her. I was jealous as well as lonesome, for I had no mother to go home to. I did have Aunt Bertha, and I thought a lot about a trip to Portland to see her. The thought didn't particularly cheer me though, and I didn't have such a flow of cash I could spend it on an airline ticket. Also, since I had worked at the church and school such a short time, I doubted if they would pay me for time off. Even so, I thought about asking for a vacation and it seemed coincidental that I would get a letter from Aunt Bertha that week. However, her second paragraph shot down any plans I might have made to go home.

I hope you won't be hurt to learn that I GOT MARRIED! I know you will remember Roger Timm,

107

the man who owned the hardware store in our shopping
center. I've known him since high school, and we've
been seeing a lot of each other since you moved to
Los Angeles. I didn't tell you about it before, because
it seemed ridiculous at my age. But he is a fine man
(and rich!) and he really seems to love me.

When you get this, dear, we will be on a *six-week
cruise!* Can you imagine your old Auntie in such a
romantic setting as an ocean liner cruising the
Carribean? I'll write you often—

There was another page, but I put the letter down. I was
happy for my aunt. But it settled the question of whether or
not I would take a trip to Portland.

The days settled into a quiet, summer routine. I went to the
office at 8:30 but left about 3:30 or 4:00 in the afternoon. Some
days I ate lunch at home with Esther; sometimes I had a hamburger with Roy and Beverly.

Richard was seldom around at lunch time. His house calls
and hospital visits were time consuming and, although the
children and teachers were on vacation, Richard worked harder
than ever trying to keep up church attendance which always
lagged in the summer.

As a consequence, I had plenty of work to do, too. At least
once a month, he dictated a letter to the congregation which
had to be mimeographed, folded, stuffed in envelopes which
had to be run through the address machine, then stamped and
mailed. There was usually at least one flyer or handbill each
month which I had to design, type and mimeograph. We also
put out a weekly newsletter, most of which Richard dictated.
It also had to be cut on a stencil and run on the mimeograph.

I asked Richard once if the church had considered some of
the more modern reproduction methods, but he quickly told
me the church couldn't afford any new office machines at this
time.

Attendance cards were another one of my jobs. Members
and visitors were encouraged to sign them on Sundays, then it
was my job to arrange them alphabetically, separate the visitor
cards and send welcome letters to first-timers. Also, members'
attendance had to be recorded.

A lot of my work couldn't be forecast. Much of my time was spent on the telephone, either taking items for the bulletin or listening to some tale of woe. Part of my time was spent playing hostess to visitors who were waiting to see Richard. The work was indeed varied, some of it hard, but none of it boring. Nevertheless, I had the feeling I was waiting.

Waiting for what? For Roy to make another advance? Waiting for some clue that would identify the person who hit me? I constantly looked for something that would open up the mysteries of who had stolen the money and who had locked me in the bell tower.

So far, my chief suspect for everything was Harry. Harry was the one who had let me out of the tower that day, and he was the one who found me on the playground. Harry also carried a tremendous bunch of keys and he easily could have one for the safe. But why would he want to put the pastor in a bad light? He seemed to like Richard. In fact, he and Esther both hovered over Richard and Dickie like parents and grandparents.

Always when I tried to figure a reason for the stolen money, the small amount puzzled me. A hundred dollars wasn't enough to make anyone risk his reputation—certainly not Richard or Gerald Loop—and I didn't believe Harry would bother with such a small amount, either.

Whenever I thought of other possible suspects in the church, I always came up against the fact that whoever had stolen the money probably locked me in the tower, and knocked me out on the playground, because I had bragged that I intended to help clear the pastor's name.

So, who knew my intention? Shirley, Roy, Beverly, Richard, Harry, Esther and Vanessa. I wrinkled my nose at the thought of Vanessa. I detested that woman (Lord, forgive me)!

As often happens, when you are thinking of someone that person appears. Vanessa came into my office without warning. I hadn't heard the door open and I was startled when I looked up and there she was.

As usual, she was impeccably groomed—not a curl out of place, not a wrinkle in her white slacks. She was beautiful— as a snowcapped mountain is beautiful.

"Hi, Louise," she spoke down to me. "Is Richard in?"

"I'm sorry, Vanessa, but you just missed him. This is his day to broadcast for the Mission."

"Oh." She frowned and put her dainty fist to her mouth. "How could I have forgotten?" She turned toward the door and then swung back. "What time is he on?"

"Eleven-thirty." I looked at my watch. "Forty-five minutes from now." She sat down, leaned back and sighed deeply. "What luck!"

She stuck out her full lips and made a sucking sound. "I wanted to get him to go have a seafood lunch. I've been hungry for a good fish dinner for days."

"We had a really good seafood dinner a couple of weeks ago," I said before I thought.

She looked mildly interested. "Where did you go?"

"I've forgotten the name, but it was at the beach, and there was an old boat in the yard."

"Probably the Sea Horse," she nodded her head. "That is a good place. Who went with you?"

Now I'd done it. All these weeks I had taken great care to put forth the image of an efficient church secretary with no male interests. To my knowledge, even Shirley didn't know how I felt about Roy, and I certainly didn't want to give the congregation an opportunity for gossip by having it known that I went to a restaurant with the pastor, even if his son did go along.

But here was Vanessa, staring at me, waiting for an answer.

I drew a deep breath, lifted my chin slightly and stared back, unblinking. I spoke coldly, formally.

"Pastor Fitzsimmons took Dickie and me one evening when Esther was too ill to prepare dinner."

Her eyes narrowed and her lips tightened. I saw a spark of anger in her eyes and felt a little afraid.

"How charming," she said and I knew I had good reason to be afraid. She tapped her fingernails on the chair arm a moment, then leaned forward. Her eyes looked wide and innocent and there wasn't a trace of frown on her smooth face, but her voice was deadly.

"Listen to me, my dear Louise. I don't know what your

110

plans are, and I've never understood why a young and pretty woman would give up a promising career in a law firm to come to a moldy, old church office, but let me make this abundantly clear. If you have any idea of taking Richard away from me, *for-get-it.*" Her eyes seemed to turn to blue steel. She leaned back then and tipped her head up imperiously.

"I've made my plans carefully and I've worked hard. I intend to be the next Mrs. Richard Fitzsimmons." She focused on me again. "So stay out of my way."

I stared at her. I couldn't believe she would talk this way. I felt myself blushing, and my heart pounded in my throat.

I looked at her tanned arms. She was slender, but in perfect condition. She could have been the one who attacked me that night on the playground. But why? And how would she know I would appear at that time? Anyway, if she was so in love with Richard that she intended to marry him, she should welcome my efforts to find out who really robbed the safe. Yet, she might just be so jealous of me, she would try to scare me away.

The thought of me being a *femme fatale* almost made me smile. But I had to remember: one, I was a woman; two, I was Richard's secretary; and three, I did live in his house. I was probably with him more than anyone else, so maybe she really was jealous of me.

"My dear Mrs. Hamilton," I could also be sarcastic, "my relationship with Reverend Fitzsimmons is entirely professional. I have no thoughts of him or for him other than loyalty to him as my employer, and respect for him as my pastor and a minister of the gospel."

She stood up and put her shoulders back. Why would she be jealous of anyone when she had a figure like that, I wondered. Her unblinking gaze made me think of Dickie's lizards.

"I'm going home so I can hear Richard's message," she said. Elegantly, she strolled to the door, then turned.

"And, Louise, remember what I said." Her eyes looked straight into mine. "Richard belongs to me."

After she was gone I jumped up and slammed a file drawer shut.

"You old bag!" I grated. I was furious. But why did I care?

Like Shirley said months ago, maybe they deserved each other.

But I did care. I suddenly realized if Richard married Vanessa, she would be Dickie's mother. The thought of him calling her mom made tears spring to my eyes. I wiped them away and blew my nose.

"This is ridiculous!" I said aloud and sat down at my desk. I forced myself to concentrate on the day's work and forgot about Richard's radio message until he had already started.

His warm, deep voice flowed out of my little transistor, bringing words of encouragement to the men on skid row. I could hear them coughing in the background as Richard told them of God's love:

"Your families may have forgotten you, but God hasn't." Richard didn't sound preachy. He sounded as though he was talking face-to-face with a group of friends.

"You've heard this message before, but try this morning to believe that God Almighty loves you so much that He decided to trade His Son's life for *yours*. Believe it, because it's true."

Part of me listened to his message, but I was also feeling the warmth of his voice and thinking of the way he looked. He was a wonderful man. No wonder Vanessa wanted him. Did I want him, too?

After his message, I snapped off the transistor and began to pick through my work. I had to accomplish something before lunch.

Esther, Harry and I were just finishing lunch when Richard came in the front door. Esther jumped up, opened the refrigerator and brought out a hamburger patty.

"Hi," Richard said. "Sorry I'm late, but I came back as soon as I could." He smiled all around, but it seemed to me he gave me a special look. "Esther, don't fix much. I'll wash and be right back."

When he came back, he had taken off his coat and tie and was drying his hands on a towel. He looked at me.

"Did you hear the broadcast?"

"Oh, yes! I thought you sounded super." We looked at each other and I had the same sinking sensation inside I had experienced in Roy's office.

"I heard ya too, Pastor," Esther said, "and I'm jest so

proud of ya." She put the patty in the frying pan. "You sure ought to have a daily radio program."

He grinned at her.

"Well, thanks, Esther, but I don't think I could take it, preparing a radio message every day, plus my church duties."

Harry was sitting at the table, picking his teeth with a toothpick. He stood up then and stretched. There were huge wet spots on his shirt under each arm.

"Speakin' of duties, I gotta get back to mine," he said.

"How's your work going, Harry?" Richard asked. He draped the hand towel over a chair and sat down beside me.

"Oh, all right." Harry's little eyes darted back and forth. "Never a dull moment, they say."

"I thought you'd be getting caught up, with school out, but it seems like you're as busy as ever. Even busy at nights."

Harry looked startled.

"Nights?" he repeated.

"Well, there have been a few times recently when I've put my car away and your camper has been gone."

Harry looked quickly at Esther who seemed unconcerned. She turned the hamburger over and took a bun out of the package.

"Last week ya had to go get paint after supper, Harry, remember?" she said. "And there was one night recently when ya went to see one of your old army buddies down to Veteran's Hospital."

Harry let out his breath.

"Oh, yeah. And then some nights I do have ta work. I been doing extra work over in Fellowship Hall. I intend to get that whole floor sanded and varnished this summer." He broke his toothpick and tossed it in his plate.

"Well, I'll see you folks later. Bye, honey," he said to Esther. He kissed her on the cheek.

"Ya be careful, honey," she said.

She pointed with her spatula, "Pastor, there's salad. Start on that and I'll have this hamburger in a jiffy."

He took the salad bowl and raked it all on his plate.

"Oh, oh," he said and smiled at me. He closed his eyes and I stared at him as he silently thanked the Lord. His eyelashes were long and black and for that moment his face was free of all lines and shadows. He looked like a boy, almost pathetic. I wanted to touch him, but was embarrassed at my feelings.

I jumped up when he opened his eyes. "I've got a lot of work to do, Richard. I'm afraid I didn't get much done this morning."

"And here's your hamburger," Esther said.

"Wait a minute, Louise," he said, then turned to Esther. "Where's Dickie?"

"The Blakelys invited him for lunch and to go swimmin', " she said. "I thought it would be all right for him to go because Mr. Blakely's going to be home today, and he can watch over the boys."

The Blakelys were the closest neighbors we had and lived in a big home next to the church property on the parsonage side. They were sophisticated and rich and showed no interest in either the church or the school, but because Dickie was the same age as their son, they often invited him over. Richard didn't always let him go, and I wondered now if he would be displeased. He smiled absently and nodded his head. Then he looked up at me.

"Why don't you sit back down and stay with me while I eat my lunch?" He pointed to my chair and I sat down like a little girl with her daddy. "So! You didn't get much done this morning," he teased, "well, 'when the cat's away, the mice will play.' "

"I wasn't playing," I said defensively. "I kept having interruptions." I wanted to tell him about Vanessa. What I wouldn't give to tell him what I really thought of her!

"I know," he said kindly, but there was a twinkle in his eye. "Of course, when a girl is as pretty as you are, you just have to expect a steady stream of people coming in to stare."

He smiled widely and I knew he was joking, but his remark pleased and flustered me so much that I knocked over the salt shaker. Richard laughed loudly and I blushed, of course.

"What's the matter, Louise?" he laughed. "Didn't you know you're pretty?"

"Pretty late to work," I quipped and stood up. "I've really got to get back."

114

As I went out the back door he called, "I'll be over as soon as I eat. I'll have to look into all those interruptions."

13

At my desk I couldn't settle down to any job. I filed a few papers, started to alphabetize the attendance cards, got up and sharpened my pencils. I opened my purse, took out my compact and looked at myself. My hands were shaking. What was the matter with me? I knew the answer. I was waiting for Richard to come.

I snapped the compact shut and groaned. Was it possible to be in love with two people at once? Or had so many terrible things happened to me I was on the verge of a nervous breakdown? Maybe I had already gone crazy. If only I could talk to someone!

Most people in trouble can go to their pastor, but how could I tell Richard my problem? *He* was the problem. If only I could really trust him. I wondered what he would do if I told him, word for word, what Vanessa had said this morning. But, that was just something else I would have to keep to myself. She could get me fired, and now with Aunt Bertha married, where could I go?

When Richard strode into the office, I jumped.

"Hey! Am I that frightening?" He grinned at me.

"Of course not." I tittered self-consciously. "I guess I'm extra nervous today." He stood in front of me, frowning.

"How come?"

"I don't know." I shrugged. I looked up at him and then out the window. "It's just that—I try not to think about the day I got locked in, but now that the kids are out of school and it's so quiet—with no one around—I imagine I hear things. Unconsciously, I touched the spot on my head where I had been hit.

"Say, how is that bump?" he asked. "All right now?"

"It's almost gone. It's been over two weeks."

"It's still a mystery to me how you could fall and bump the

top of your head."

Impulsively, I decided this was the time to talk to him. I had to confide in someone. I couldn't go on alone any longer with these thoughts.

He went to his desk and sat down. I walked in after him and closed the door. He looked up, surprised when I sat down in the chair for visitors. It was placed next to his desk, facing him.

"Richard, may I talk to you? Could you forget I'm your secretary and think of me as one of the church members who needs counseling?"

His expression was grave, but soft, encouraging. He leaned back in his chair and folded his arms across his chest.

"What's the trouble, Louise?"

"First of all, you told me yourself you thought my being locked in the tower had something to do with you, remember?" He nodded. "Well, I think there's more going on around here than you realize. First of all, I haven't told you about the cats."

"The cats?"

"Not real ones—cartoon cats—drawings. The first one was stuck under the door the day I got locked in. It was a childish drawing of a dead cat with the word 'Curiosity' under it. It was on a scrap of paper."

He jerked his head back in disbelief.

"Then the night on the playground I got the second one."

"How do you mean, you got the second one?"

"Remember, you told me to get ready for bed and that you would come in to check on me? When I got undressed, the drawing of the cat fell out of my clothes. Whoever hit me—"

"Hit you?"

"Richard, I *know* someone hit me. I didn't fall and bounce around on top of my head."

He twisted his mouth to one side and frowned.

"Anyway, whoever hit me must have put that drawing in my clothes."

"But that means—who could have known you would be out there?"

"I've thought of that, and nobody could have known, because *I* didn't know I'd be out there. The person must really want to scare me, and was prepared. I mean—ready with another cat drawing."

He looked out the window and rubbed his chin. I couldn't tell what he was thinking. He shook his head back and forth.

"It sounds unreal."

"I know. I think that, too, until I look at the drawings."

"Where are they?"

"In my jewel box. I'll show them to you tonight." He nodded, and then cleared his throat.

"Louise, tell me what you believe happened that night. Who do you think hit you?" His eyes had a peculiar glint in them.

"For awhile I honestly thought it was Harry, but—

"Why did you think it was Harry?"

If only I could quit trembling! I hugged myself in an effort to quit shaking, both inside and out. Richard had a terrible effect on me. I wanted to be with him, yet he scared me. I wanted to tell him all my fears and longings, but did I dare? What if I was wrong to put all my trust in him?

"I thought it was Harry at first because I saw him with another man that night in the storeroom."

"What!" Richard's mouth was slightly open and his eyes wide. "Who was the other man?"

"I don't know because I could only see his back."

"What were they doing?"

"I don't know. They were talking about a camera, and there was all kinds of stuff on the floor, like radios and record players—"

Richard gaped at me.

"I sort of lost my balance—I was peeking in the window—I made a noise and then they shut the venetian blind. I was scared then so I ran back to the house—"

"Louise, Louise, *why* didn't you tell me this before? You know there have been robberies around here. Why, that sounds to me as if old Harry is in pretty deep."

"I didn't tell you because I hoped there was a logical explanation, and besides, I was afraid. I *am* afraid. I don't want to be hurt again. But the main reason I don't think Harry is the one, is because—pardon my frankness—I think I would have smelled him!"

Richard leaned back and laughed loudly. He laughed until he had to wipe his eyes and blow his nose. I laughed, too.

After he quit laughing, I told him all the rest, about seeing Harry's camper, watching them move the TV into the storeroom, and going out there the second time.

"I'm almost positive they didn't see or hear me that time. I think there was someone else on the playground that night, and that person—Mr. X—is the one who has it in for you Richard, and the one who locked me in the tower, and knocked me out on the playground."

Richard leaned back and his chair squawked. He sighed deeply.

"Incredible," he murmured.

"So, this is why I wanted to talk to you," I explained. "I really am afraid."

"You have good reason," he said, and rocked his chair slightly.

I still hadn't said anything about my personal emotions, but before I could even think how to say it, I blurted out, "And, Richard, besides all this, I'm afraid I'm in love with you."

He stopped rocking. I think he actually stopped breathing. The room became so quiet I could hear the small whirring of an electric clock on his desk. At last he leaned forward, rested his arms on the glass top and locked his fingers together. He looked directly into my eyes and my heart beat in such a heavy rhythm, I could scarcely breathe.

"Louise, you're so young. You've lost your fiance, your mother died, and you simply need someone to love. I'm flattered, as any man would be, to think a young and beautiful girl could love me, but I'm much too old for you."

"No! No, you're not! I *know* how I feel. I do love you."

He swung his chair so he faced the window. He spoke without looking at me and his voice was a monotone.

"Don't think I haven't been aware of you. But it has only been eight months since Vera died. She—she meant everything to me. So, I know anything I feel for you is the product of my loneliness."

I could feel the hot misery of tears being born. I felt humiliated. I wanted to run away, out into some field where I could cry and scream. But I sat there and looked down at my hands. Silently, the tears began to slip down my cheeks and into my lap. I had to sniff. He turned and faced me then.

"Louise, please don't cry. You have your whole life ahead of you. I'm sure the Lord has just the right man for you."

I lifted my head defiantly.

"And I'm sure the Lord has just the right woman for you! Vanessa!"

"What are you talking about?"

"She told me this morning she intends to have you. She told me to keep my hands off, that you belong to her!"

He look startled, then bewildered. At last a smile began to tremble at the edge of his lips. He began to chuckle, and then I had to smile, too.

"I was warned about things like this in seminary, but—" he began to laugh, almost out of control, "but it's the first time it's happened to me!"

Without knowing why, I began to cry again. He stood up and hurried around the desk. He put his arms around me and I could feel the heat of his body. He tipped my chin up and I tried to look away. I knew my nose was red and snuffly, and I knew he was only being kind. My tears tasted salty as I licked my lips.

"Louise," he whispered. His face was so close it was like seeing him through a magnifying glass. "If our feelings for each other are on the rebound—so be it." He kissed me gently at first, then hungrily. Suddenly, he eased me away. He cleared his throat and turned his back to me.

"We're going to have to establish some ground rules." He stepped to the door and opened it. "The first rule is, never to be in a closed room together."

My heart seemed to be bursting with happiness. He loved me!

"No matter how we feel, or *think* we feel, the work here, our dedication to the Lord Jesus has to come first." He looked stern, almost angry.

"There must not be even a hint of scandal from this office," he continued, and took a few paces around the room, smacked his hands together, then stood by the window.

"If I seem cold or gruff, Louise, it's only to keep myself in check." He turned toward me and I thought for a breathless moment he would take me in his arms again, but his shoulders sagged a little.

"You'll have to help me, Louise. At least until Vera—" he didn't finish the sentence.

"I understand," I said. I was so glad I had told him all my fears and longings. He cared for me and now I wasn't alone.

"We still haven't solved the problems around here," he said. "I don't know what to do about Harry. If I confront him, it may put you in more danger. I think I'll walk over to the store-room right now and see what's in there."

"Oh, Richard, be careful!" I called after him. My voice sounded thin. "Shouldn't you call the police?"

"If there's a logical explanation, it would be embarrassing to call the police," he answered. "And think how it would hurt Esther." He stood at the door and looked at me. There was that sinking sensation again.

"I'll see you in a little bit," he said softly.

And once again I was alone in the empty church building.

14

I sat with my arms on the typewriter, my head down for a few moments after Richard left. I didn't want to work. All I wanted to do was think about him, but the work on my desk had to be done and I decided I might as well face it.

I sat up straight and looked at the overflowing "In" basket. I hated to get behind. Vanessa's unwelcome visit, and listening to the pastor's radio message had cancelled my morning, and so far this afternoon. . .my mind was on Richard again!

I leaned back in my chair and looked out the window. The rose bushes were in full bloom. Their red, pink, orange and white blossoms basked in the hot afternoon sun. It seemed as though the whole world was taking a nap. As I sat there day-dreaming about Richard, Roy's face appeared in my mind— his expressive, brilliant eyes, and his handsome features.

I wondered—if I could have either Richard or Roy, which

one would I choose? Roy was romantic, amusing and had a terrific personality. I could always be sure of a good time with him with his joking, singing and general good humor. There was no denying something about him stirred me.

But Richard! He was like a harbor, and his kiss thrilled me more than any kiss I had ever experienced. Was it because he was older?

I had been rolling a pencil back and forth in my fingers. Suddenly, I threw it across the room.

"Probably neither of them love me!" I said aloud. "If I keep on wasting time, I'm going to lose my job!" Ashamed of my tantrum, I got up, picked up the pencil, and determined to get to work.

I had just rolled paper and carbons in the typewriter when I heard it—a muffled, scraping sound directly overhead.

I looked up, but could only see a high, cream-colored ceiling trimmed with dark wood molding. I followed the molding around the room until I saw either a furnace vent or an air vent in the ceiling. I had never noticed it before, but while I was looking at it, I heard the cautious, scraping sound again. It seemed to come directly from the vent.

I felt the hair stand up at the back of my neck and goose bumps appeared on my arms. Someone was up there. For a moment, it seemed all the life in my body drained out. My arms felt heavy and I couldn't move. Then reason took over.

Of course there was someone up there. It was probably Harry doing some kind of special summer maintenance. Didn't he say he was going to try to get the rooms painted this summer? So he was probably moving furniture in the sixth grade room. Gradually life seemed to come back into my body and I began again to transcribe my shorthand. After every sentence or two, I would quit typing and listen, but all I could hear was the sound of my electric typewriter's motor.

It was almost four o'clock when Richard finally came back.

"Any calls?" he asked in a businesslike tone. I looked at him for some special sign, but his face was impersonal. It hurt my feelings. I didn't expect him to throw his arms around me, but after what had happened between us, I thought at least his eyes would speak to me.

"No calls, Reverend Fitzsimmons." He stopped short and looked at me, then a faint smile appeared at one corner of his mouth. We both laughed and he popped me lightly on top of the head with his open hand.

"Ow!" I yelped. "Don't forget my concussion."

"Poor, awkward child," he said. As he started toward the study, he turned back. "By the way, I saw Harry this afternoon. He was working in the storeroom."

"Did you see anything like stereos or cameras?"

"Not a thing. Looked just like it always has. Dusty, paint cans, ladders."

"Well, I guess he and that other man got rid of everything as soon as possible." Richard looked at me through narrowed eyes, with a teasing smile on his lips.

"Louise, are you sure what you saw? I mean, a work bench and a few cans of paint with a drop cloth over it might look—"

I became instantly furious.

"I KNOW what I saw!"

"Okay!" He put his hands out as though to soothe me. "Old Harry was trying to get the sander working. I helped him a little and we talked, oh, maybe twenty minutes. He seems like a good old boy. It's hard to imagine him in any sort of intrigue."

"Richard!" I gasped. "Did you say Harry was over in the storeroom all afternoon?" Quickly I told him about the scraping noise upstairs. "Someone was up there, and it couldn't have been Harry!"

Richard's calm look was maddening.

"How about Roy?" he asked. "Couldn't he be upstairs for some reason? After all, he's the principal of the school—he has the right to be anywhere." He smiled at me as though I was about four years old.

"But Roy's not even here today. He told me to take his calls because he had to go to the dentist, and Bev has taken the afternoon off."

"Esther?" he said, but I shook my head.

"Maybe it was a branch scraping the building."

"Oh, Richard!" I slapped my hand down on the desk. "There's not the slightest wind stirring any branches."

He smiled and shrugged. "Ghosts?" He laughed then and went into his office. The latch clicked a finish to our conversation.

But I was certain someone had been in the room above. Determined, I left my desk, hurried down the hall past Bev's office, out the door and upstairs. I ran the distance along the outside balcony to the sixth grade room. In front of the door with my hand on the knob, my heart pounded. My lips were compressed as I resolutely turned the knob. It was locked. Relieved, yet frustrated, I turned and started back toward the stairs. Across the yard, Harry was just coming out of the storeroom. He looked up at me and waved.

From this height, I could see the Blakelys' pool. There were several children in it but I couldn't tell which one was Dickie. The sun was a white-hot ball and I hoped he wouldn't get sunburned. I looked at my watch and sighed. Four o'clock and my work was not yet finished.

The next day when Jerry brought the mail, I was excited to find a yellow and orange flowered envelope with a return, "Shirley Bennett." I could hardly wait to open it. The phone rang, "Arboleda Heights Christian Church," I said.

"Hello! Hello!" I answered, louder each time. Did I hear a sigh? I put the phone back carefully. The line must be out of order, but I began to tremble, and it wasn't easy to open Shirley's letter.

Hello, friend. I've thought of you muchly since I got home, but there just hasn't been time to write. This is a vacation?

But I decided I had to take time to write after Roy and his weird roommate (I did NOT like him) came to see me last night. Roy came down to San Diego on the pretense of giving me samples of a new curriculum, but I got the feeling that wasn't the real reason for his visit.

He hinted around that Rev. Fitz was acting stranger than ever, and that *you* seemed thin and exhausted. What is that man doing to you??? Could you get

123

away for a weekend and come tell me what's happening? You could get the bus right there in Arboleda Hts. and I'll meet you here. Please come, dear Louise. I'd love for you to meet Mother, and we could go to the beach and to Mission Bay. I might even manage to get a sailor for you!

Seriously, dear friend, please be careful. I can't remember how Roy said it, but he said something about you being in *danger??* He said you needed to get away for a rest. I thought he was kidding, but the more I think about it, I'm convinced he was serious. *Is* anything wrong? Watch your step, okay? Why don't you get Harry to put a chain lock on your room door? *I'm serious.* ANSWER NOW, AND TELL ME YOU'RE COMING!

In Christ,
Shirl

I put Shirley's letter down and leaned forward on the typewriter. I could feel my fingers trembling and I held out my hands to look at them. Shaky as an old lady's! I bit my lower lip. If I had known how scary it was going to be at this gruesome old church, I would never have come. But then, I would never have met Roy, or Richard, or Shirley.

I picked up her letter and read it again. Could I go to Shirley's for a weekend? The thought of going somewhere on a bus, being at the beach with my good friend, laughing, talking, playing in the ocean, seemed overwhelmingly exciting. But did I want to be away from Richard that long?

I closed my eyes and, without warning, I relived yesterday's kiss and felt thrilled all over again. I allowed myself then to daydream a love scene: Richard took me in his arms, looked deep into my eyes and said, "Louise, darling! I can't live without you. Marry me."

I opened my eyes. Would I marry him? Another question exploded in my mind, disintegrating all romantic thoughts. Why did Vera kill herself? Why? If Richard was the wonderful person he seemed to be, how could she have made the decision to leave him? No. There had to be something wrong.

There had to be a reason.

The still office seemed cold and I shivered. Maybe I *would* go to Shirley's for a weekend.

Roy came in just then, businesslike, a bulging folder in his hands.

"Hi, Louise. I hate to ask you to do Bev's work," he began. He placed the folder on my desk and flipped it open. He picked up a sheet and placed it on my desk. "But I've got to have this information dittoed and in the mail this week. It's about fall registration, and Beverly's sick."

"Oh, no," I said. "What's wrong with her?"

"Oh, stomach flu I think she said, or summer flu. Whatever. She'll be okay in a day or so, but I've got to have this."

Our eyes met and held—but I felt nothing! I still liked him, even felt affectionate toward him, but the thrill was gone. I was really fickle, I decided—or unstable.

I picked up the sheet and read it quickly.

"I'll be glad to do this for you right now," I said and smiled widely. Somehow I felt guilty for not being in love with him anymore.

I looked down, saw Shirley's letter and remembered her warning. I tried to look stern.

"Hey—what's this about you telling Shirley I'm worn out and in danger?" It seemed to take him off guard and his mouth opened slightly.

In that moment, I realized there was no way for Roy to have known I was in danger that night on the playground, unless Richard had told him, and I didn't see how Richard could have because Roy was at the dentist yesterday afternoon and the pastor had left early this morning to go to Long Beach.

Roy glanced down at the brightly flowered envelope, picked it up and read the return.

"Oh, good," he said, smiling. "She wrote to you already." He looked down at me with clear, honest eyes. "Now don't get shook up, okay? But Louise, I really believe you are in danger."

My heart began to thud.

"Roy, I wish you wouldn't kid around about things like that! This place scares me enough anyway."

"I'm not kidding." His jaw lifted slightly and he jammed his hands down into his pants pockets. He turned away and looked at the pastor's study door.

"I'm not going to put in words what I know, because it has to do with 'wickedness in high places.' " He looked directly at me. His tongue darted out and touched his lower lip.

"Louise, it would be good if you spent this weekend away from here. Go on down to Shirley's. Please." His heavy brown eyebrows were drawn together, his manner was compassionate.

"It would probably be better for you if you'd quit this job altogether and go back to your lawyers in Portland."

"Roy!" I was indignant, yet scared. "I think you're trying to tell me to get lost."

He sat down on the corner of my desk and tipped my chin up with his finger. A week ago, two days ago, I would have turned to jelly inside if he had been this close, but today he was just a friend. He didn't seem to be as handsome as I had thought. His heavy-lidded, romantic look seemed almost humorous to me now.

"You know I would never tell you to get lost," he whispered. "I just don't want you to get hurt."

"Who would hurt me, Roy?" I gently pulled away from him and opened the stationery drawer for a ditto master.

"I told you I didn't want to name names. Just trust me, and be careful." He stood up, walked over to the window, put his hands in his pockets and jiggled his change.

With sweaty hands, I rolled the master in the typewriter. I flipped the switch and lightly rested my fingers on the keys. One finger suddenly struck the "d" key.

"Oh, rats!" I whined. "See what you've made me do, Roy? You've got me so nervous."

"I'm sorry, Louise. I didn't mean for you to get upset. But let me say one more thing." He took a deep breath and put the tips of his fingers together.

"Now you aren't going to like what I say." He faced me with a wide-eyed stare. "But I know you. You're still determined to make a hero out of you-know-who." He motioned toward the study. "But you're putting your confidence in the wrong person."

I felt my jaw tense and an angry feeling began somewhere in my chest. But I kept silent. My face began to get red.

"Now I see I've made you angry," he said. He lifted his palms. "All right—all right. Believe what you want to." He took another deep breath through his nose, and his nostrils flared.

"Well, now, you say you can get that thing done this morning?" I nodded. "Good. I'll be back for it after awhile."

He walked quickly out the door, turned and spoke gravely. "Louise, if you need me, for *anything,* yell!"

15

When Roy came back for the letter, I said, "Roy, I've decided to go to Shirley's this weekend."

His blue eyes widened and then he smiled. "Good girl! The change will do you good."

As soon as he left the office, I called the bus depot for the schedule of departures, then called Shirley.

"You're really coming?" She sounded excited. "Oh! We'll have fun, I promise you!" I had just put the phone down when Richard came in. I reached for my purse.

"Richard, I just made a long distance call. Should I put some money in Petty Cash or give it to you?"

He shrugged and smiled at me. His dark eyes were soft and lingering, and I had to struggle to keep my mind on what he was saying.

"It doesn't matter. Did you talk long?"

"Not more than three minutes, I don't think. I called Shirley in San Diego."

"Oh?" He look mildly inquisitive. "Well, why don't you wait until the bill comes, then you can give Gerald Loop the exact amount." He picked up his mail and fanned through it quickly. "Anything wrong with Shirley?"

I held up Shirley's letter.

"No, but she invited me to come down for the weekend."

"This weekend?"

"Is it all right? I told her I'd come Friday afternoon."

He frowned slightly and pursed his lips.

"It's all right. The only thing is I had planned to be gone this weekend, too."

I looked at him in surprise. I usually knew his plans.

"I didn't mention it," he explained, "because the fewer people who know, the better church attendance is."

I saw the color come into his face. "I don't mean for that to sound as though I'm the great drawing card." He seemed embarrassed. "But it does work out that way."

Why hadn't he confided in me? It hurt my feelings. He must have read my thoughts because he said, "I should have told you, Louise. You aren't a gossip." His eyes seemed to ask my forgiveness.

"That's okay," I said. "Do you want me to call Shirley and tell her I can't come?"

"Of course not. There's no need for that. But I am sorry you'll miss hearing Roy preach."

"Oh, no! I've always wanted to hear him preach. And besides—Dickie will be alone. I'll call Shirley now and cancel." He put his hand firmly over mine as I reached for the phone.

"No, no." He looked stern. "Esther can take care of Dickie. You go on and have a weekend with Shirley. You don't have enough fun for a girl your age, anyway."

"Where are you going?" I asked, stammering. Our eyes met and held. "This weekend, I mean?"

"An old seminary buddy of mine was scheduled to speak at a laymen's retreat at Pine Tree Lodge, but he had to have emergency surgery. He asked me to take his place." He smiled. "I'm looking forward to it."

He opened the study door, then came back a step or two. "Isn't the VBS Committee having a dinner Friday night?"

I whirled around in my chair and looked at the church calendar.

"Yes—six p.m., Fellowship Hall."

"Well—it would be good if one of us could be there for it—"

"Of course! I'll call Shirley and cancel—it's okay!"

"No you don't! I'll have Roy go. You go right ahead."

I worked hard the rest of the week, and by Friday afternoon, my "In" basket was empty.

Richard drove me to the bus depot. Any hope I had nourished about a romantic farewell vanished when he pulled up to the curb in front of the depot.

"This is an unloading zone, Louise, so if you don't mind—"

I jumped out and picked up my small overnight case.

"See you Monday," he called and pulled out into traffic. I watched the brown station wagon until it disappeared.

Shirley was waiting for me at the depot in San Diego, but I almost walked by her. Her hair was cut short and her skin was dark brown. Her teeth and the whites of her eyes seemed blue-white in contrast. We embraced warmly and I could smell a spicy carnation scent. We looked at each other and giggled.

"Oh, Louise," she cried, squeezing me around the waist, "we're going to have so much fun!" She led the way to her little white Nova. I felt a happy warmth and excitement in being with her again.

"And guess what?" She turned to look at me with her mischievous, brown eyes. "We've got dates tonight!"

I was appalled. A date? I didn't want a date, unless it could be with Richard. But I couldn't let Shirley know how I felt about him. He had said that nothing was to interfere with the Lord's work, so I couldn't confide in her, or anyone, until he was ready to tell it himself. I smiled brightly.

"A date? Oh, no! Who?"

"My cousin and a friend!" She drove expertly through the city and I tried to sight-see and pay attention to her at the same time. "You'll be with my cousin, Glen, and Louise, he's neat. A little short, but really a great guy, and I'll be with his friend, Tony."

The evening was fun. They took us to a seafood restaurant with lots of atmosphere, and I thought of Richard and Dickie and the night we had dined on seafood. After dinner, they took us to Mission Bay. We got on a steamboat, listened to Dixieland music, drank Cokes and laughed a lot.

Glen, as short as Shirley had said, was a nice fellow, but immature compared to Richard. I kept thinking of Richard all evening, and prayed that the Lord would keep him safe and be with him as he spoke to the men at the retreat. How I wished he was with me as I looked out at the moonlit bay!

Finally, the evening was over and the three of them made plans to take me to the beach the next day. Shirley's mother, Mrs. Bennett, had opened up the couch in the den for me, but Shirley and I talked until about three in the morning.

The ringing of a phone woke me, and I couldn't remember where I was. I sat up and looked around at the strange room. Mrs. Bennett answered the telephone, then came to my room.

"Louise, dear, it's for you."

Fear went through me like a knife. Richard!

I snatched up my robe and was still trying to poke my arms in the sleeves when I got to the phone in the dining room. Mrs. Bennett went on into the kitchen.

"Hello!" My voice was shrill.

"Louise, honey, this is Esther." My heart was beating in my throat. "Hope I didn't scare you."

"What's wrong?"

"Well, honey, maybe nothin'. And then again, maybe everythin'. I don't know what to make of it, and I jest felt like ya ought to know. Harry seemed to think I was making somethin' out of—"

"Esther, what is it?" My face felt tight and my mouth dry.

"You know last night was the VBS dinner?"

"Uh-huh."

"Well, one of the ladies, I can't think of her name, she was asking Roy, Mr. Decker, where the pastor was and Mr. Decker, he grinned like it was some kinda joke, and sorta shrugged his shoulders."

I could visualize Roy's prankish look, but why would he do that?

"Maybe you didn't hear the woman's question," I said.

"Oh, I most certainly heard her right. I was standin' right next ta her. And then she said, 'Louise isn't here either,' and, instead of Mr. Decker explaining where you were, he jest kept on a-grinnin' ornerylike."

"Didn't you tell her?" I cut in impatiently.

"Well, I said, 'Now, Mr. Decker, ya know where they're at!' but he just bowed low at the waist like he does sometimes and said, 'If you ladies will excuse me, I have to study for

130

my sermon tomorrow' and he was gone jest like that."

"You did explain to whoever it was, didn't you?" I bit my lower lip and started picking at a blemish on my cheek.

"Honey, that's jest it. That's why I called. I tried to. I said, 'Mrs.'—oh, shoot, why can't I think of her name—anyway, I started to tell her and she excused herself and said she was needed in the kitchen."

My mind grasped this information and I felt a dull sickness as I realized what it could mean. I knew the women would gossip about it, at least some of them.

"Oh, Esther," I whispered, "that's terrible! Why didn't you make her listen? That sounds as though the pastor and I are together."

"I know, darlin'—that's why I called. I tried to go find that woman, but she must have slipped out through the kitchen. I thought maybe ya ought to come home, and be in church in the mornin'."

"I'll have to talk to Shirley," I said, trying to figure out what to do. I wished I'd never heard of Arboleda Heights Christian Church and School. The thought of going to church with people staring at me, wondering if I'd spent the night with the preacher, made my cheeks burn. I couldn't seem to get a deep enough breath. As I said goodbye to Esther, I saw Shirley coming into the room. She was barefoot and in a short nightie.

"What's happening?" She yawned and scratched her shoulder sleepily.

When I looked up at her, I began to cry. I told her, sniffing and sobbing, what Esther had said. As I cried and talked, I noticed Shirley's feet.

First, her left foot rubbed her right ankle and then the other way around. Her toenails were enameled bright orange with flecks of gold. She looked comical, standing there in her short nightie, with her tousled hair, her eyes enormous with sympathy. I began to laugh hysterically. I felt as though I was going out of control. Shirley's eyes got bigger, then she reached out, grabbed my shoulders and gave me a hard shake.

"Louise! Stop it now, just STOP IT!"

"I can't help it!" I laughed, tears streaming down my cheeks.
I felt wild and somehow detached, as though I was a spectator

watching the whole scene.

"I'm sorry," I said, ashamed. I blew my nose and wiped my eyes.

"Poor kid," Shirley said and looked up at her mother. "Esther called and—"

"I heard," Mrs. Bennett said. "I doubt if it's as bad as it seems right now." I looked up at her hopefully. "Things always seem worse on an empty stomach." She laughed and patted my shoulders. "You two come on in the kitchen and I'll make pancakes."

After breakfast and a lot of talk, we decided the best way to stop any gossip was for me to go back to Los Angeles, and be in church Sunday morning.

Shirley offered to drive me, but I knew she was looking forward to going to the beach with Tony, so I refused her offer. She drove me to the bus depot and we promised each other to get together at least once more during the summer.

On the way home, I kept trying to figure out why Roy would let that woman, whoever she was, think Richard and I were together. It was so unlike him. I knew he didn't like the pastor, but he liked me. In fact, I was sure he was attracted to me. Wouldn't he try to protect my reputation? Besides, he was a talkative person. He loved to supply information, expound on any subject. Why would he say *nothing* when he knew the truth? I looked at the ocean from the bus window and felt cheated. If it hadn't been for Roy, I would be lying on the beach this minute having fun with friends my age, with the prospect of more fun tonight.

What would I do tonight? Should I call Roy and ask him for an explanation? Maybe I should invite him over for a talk and have Esther present. Then we could get everything straightened out. I would ask Esther what she thought.

It was after four o'clock in the afternoon when I finally got to the parsonage. I was hot and in a bad humor, having jolted along on a city bus for an hour, then having walked three long blocks from the bus stop.

As soon as I got in the living room, I collapsed on the couch.

"Why didn't ya call, child?" Esther clucked over me. She took off my shoes and almost ran to get a glass of iced tea.

"Harry would'a come," she said, her face lined with worry wrinkles. I rubbed my feet together and decided never to wear that pair of shoes again.

"I know Harry is extra busy on Saturdays," I said. At the bus depot I had thought about calling for a ride home, but ever since that night on the playground, I had been afraid to be alone with Harry. I didn't think he was the one who had hit me, but I believed he was in it somehow. Poor Esther, I thought. My heart went out to her as I watched her take my overnight case up the stairs. She was so sweet and good. What a shame for her to be married to a character like Harry.

Dickie came yelling in the back door and my heart seemed to have a glad welcome for him.

"Esther!" He sounded excited. "Lookit!" He came running into the living room. "Louise! You came back!" He ran to me, gave me a hug, and plopped beside me. His little face was sweat-streaked and I could smell his strong boy smell—dust, jeans and sneakers. He held his left hand almost under my nose.

"Look at this salamander!" His eyes were wild with excitement. "Did you know he's supposed to be able to live in the fire?"

I looked at the snake-like face and shuddered. "Shall we try?"

"Louise! Shame on you!" He cuddled the thing in his palms. "Poor little sally," he cooed.

"Are you going to put him—her—in your terrarium?"

"Yep," he smiled and held the lizard close to his eyes. "He's so cute!"

"Why don't you go put him where he'll be safe?" I closed my eyes and swallowed. I wasn't as afraid as I had been a few months ago, but I still didn't like Dickie's pets. "He's probably terrified in your hands, and you might drop him."

"Ooh!" He leaped off the couch and took the stairs two at a time.

"Don't forget to wash your hands!" I sounded like a mother, and the thought made me smile.

In about three minutes Dickie was back beside me, holding up his hands. There were water streaks on his dirty arms, and

I took one arm and turned it so he could see. He grinned and leaned against me. I hugged him again.

"Did you ever see our Holy Bible?"

I laughed. "Which one is that? Aren't they all holy?" He screwed up his mouth and thought about it. "Yes. But this one's *more* holy, 'cause it's bigger."

He went over to an end table and picked up a big, black Bible with gold edges. I had seen it before, but never opened it. It was so big he almost dropped it before he sank down beside me and dumped it in my lap.

"This Bible has 'corded all our birthdays," he said and quickly opened the front cover. In Vera's plain handwriting she had recorded their full names and dates of birth and the date of their wedding. In Richard's peculiar hand was the date of Vera's death. It was sad and final.

Esther came downstairs and "tsked, tsked" at Dickie.

"Can't you leave her alone, Dickie? Can't you see how tired she is?"

"It's okay, Esther. I want to see this Holy Bible." I smiled and winked at her.

"Well, all right. But, Dickie, you need a bath and if you leave the tub like you did last night—" She shook her head.

"Louise, I opened your windows and turned on the fan and cleaned up the bathroom."

"Thanks so much, dear Esther," I said as I leafed idly through the Bible. There was a beautiful picture of Moses and the burning bush, and David and Goliath.

Between the Old and New Testaments, there was a sheet from a stenographer's shorthand tablet. In Vera's handwriting was a short message. I traced the words with my index finger:

"Forgive me, but I don't know what else to do." I felt something close to horror and jerked my hand away. This was the suicide note.

Dickie was telling Esther about the salamander and so I quickly put the note down and turned the pages until I came to another illustration. But my mind wasn't on the family Bible. My thoughts were tumbling like clothes in a dryer.

I thought police kept suicide notes, but evidently not. Of course, Richard would want to keep the last thing his wife had ever written. I felt depressed and apprehensive. I closed the Bible and put it on the table.

"It's too hot to sit here, Dickie," I said and forced a smile. "I'm going to take a shower, okay?" I picked up my shoes and purse and pulled myself up the stairs.

I looked back at him. "I'll look at the Holy Bible more another time," I promised.

Something about that suicide note bothered me.

16

The water felt wonderful. I kept thinking about Vera's suicide note. What was there about it that bothered me?

I let the warm water stream through my hair and down my face. Was it odd that Vera hadn't addressed the note to Richard or to anyone? There was just that short message with no beginning and no ending. I suppose people do strange things before they kill themselves, but I was sure, if I were going to leave a note, I would have said "Dear Somebody" or "To Whom it May Concern," and I felt just as sure I would have signed my name. Another thing that bothered me was the feeling that I had seen the note before. I turned off the water and reached for a big towel.

I put on faded jeans and a tee shirt and, before I could get my hair put up on big, pink curlers, I was wet with perspiration.

I had just put the last curler in and was about to go down to the kitchen to get something to eat when I remembered where I had seen a note like the one downstairs in the Bible. I picked up my purse and loped down the stairs.

Esther and Dickie were in the kitchen putting food on the table for a cold supper, but I couldn't take time to eat right now. I ran out the back door.

"Where're ya goin', honey?" Esther called after me. "I was jest fixing us a bite to eat."

"I've got to check on something," I yelled over my shoulder. "I'll be right back."

As I ran across the playground, I could feel the hot asphalt give under my tennis shoes. I fumbled in my purse as I ran and had the keys in my hand by the time I got to the school door.

Inside, the air felt dead and hot. I hurried along the silent hallway to the office, unlocked the door and opened the window. My desk was so neat it startled me. It's funny, I thought, how hard you can work if you have a goal.

I sat down in my chair and opened the second drawer. Toward the back, under some other supplies, was the steno pad Vera had used. It only took me a second or two to find the note I was looking for.

"Dear Eunice," it said on the first line. Yes! It definitely was the same handwriting. "I'm sorry to do this, but I don't know what else to do—" The same phrase! "I'm swamped with Junior Church, working for Richard and trying to be a mother to Dickie. I simply cannot take on VBS next summer and I was won—" She had zigzagged through the whole message. On the next page she had tried again and had scratched it all. I knew the sheet in Dickie's Holy Bible had come from this notebook. I swung around in my chair and stared out the window. What did it mean? Had she become so desperate while trying to write a note to Eunice she had decided to take her life? That was possible, I guessed, but didn't seem very plausible.

Even with the window open, it was still and hot in my office, but I felt cold and my hands were clammy. A morbid, terrifying thought had formed in my mind. What if Vera had not committed suicide? What if, for some reason, she had been murdered? And what if, somehow, the murderer had come across this notebook and decided that Vera's last note to Eunice would make a perfect suicide note? Who had the easiest access to this desk? My heart sank. Richard.

I heard a slight noise at the door and whirled around. There was Roy, apparently as surprised to see me as I was to see him.

"Louise!" He tried to smile, but either he had been frightened by my presence, or distressed, because his eyes remained round and wide. "I thought you were in San Diego." He quickly recovered his composure.

I suddenly felt very put out with Roy Decker.

136

"I *am* supposed to be in San Diego, having a wonderful time, but thanks to you, I'm back at work."

"What are you talking about?"

"Esther called me this morning and said you deliberately let some woman at the dinner last night think that Richard and I had gone away together!"

His mouth dropped open innocently.

"What are you saying?"

I told him everything Esther had told me. His mouth closed tightly and he snorted.

"I don't remember anything like that," he growled. "I was probably kidding around." He made a helpless gesture. "Now why would Esther get her feathers up about that?" He looked so young and bewildered I decided he hadn't meant to put Richard and me in a bad light. I softened a little toward him.

"Well, I wish there was some way you could publicly declare we are not together," I said primly.

"Should I announce it from the pulpit?" His teasing self was back.

"Yes!" I joked with him, then asked, "What are you doing here this late?"

"I was going to ask you the same thing."

I hesitated a moment. He was staring at me, waiting for my answer, and before I thought it through, I blurted, "This afternoon I saw the suicide note."

His eyes widened slightly and he moved back a fraction of an inch.

"You mean Vera Fitzsimmons'?"

"Yes."

"Where?"

"Dickie and I were looking at the family Bible, and there it was."

He took a deep breath and looked at me sympathetically. "That must have been a shocker."

"It was shocking. But," I picked up Vera's notebook, "what's more shocking to me is the fact that I have found some notes here in Vera's shorthand tablet that are almost identical to the one in the Bible."

I flipped it open and showed the page to him. He bent over

my desk and examined it. "And see here," I continued, "she tried to reword her note to Eunice on this page."

He read them both, then read them again. His eyes darted back and forth and he touched his lips with the tip of his tongue. He looked at me with half-closed eyes.

"Well—I guess I'm dense. What are you saying?"

"These notes, Roy, they're almost identical to the one—oh! Of course you don't know what I'm talking about. You haven't seen the note in the Bible." I described it to him.

"Don't you see how odd it is for her to use almost the same wording in a note to a friend as she used in her 'farewell' letter?"

He looked at me as though he was trying to understand a foreign language. At last he said, "What do you think it means, Louise?"

I looked down at my manicured nails—especially done for San Diego. What I was thinking was too radical to put in words, and yet—maybe Roy had been right about Richard all the time. But how could anyone who seemed so dedicated to the Lord be such a hypocrite?

Memories of my first day on the job came back to me. Richard had questioned me so thoroughly about my belief in God.

"I want to be sure you're a genuine Christian," he had said.

And there were other times when he had talked about people in the congregation who hid behind a facade of respectability.

"Only God knows the real Christians," he had said. Had Richard been hiding behind the facade of a pious preacher?

I looked up at Roy's face. He jiggled coins in his pocket impatiently.

"Well? What do you think?" he said.

I sighed deeply.

"I hate to tell you. But," I held up an index finger, "I think it was strange that Vera's suicide note didn't have a salutation or a closing. She was a secretary, Roy, and I don't think she would have written even a short message without saying, 'Dear Richard' or something." Roy's face was set, his eyes narrow and his head slightly tilted.

"Also, knowing how I feel about Dickie, the more positive I

am that even if Vera contemplated suicide and wrote a note, her love for him would have compelled her to put in something special to him."

I folded my arms and leaned back. Roy continued to stare at me, lips pursed. He jiggled the coins in his pocket again.

"So, what you're saying is, you don't believe Vera took her own life." Roy's lips parted slightly and his front teeth and his bright eyes made him look a little like a squirrel. He shook his head. "What you're implying, Louise, is too serious to put into words."

"That's what I said."

We were both silent for about thirty seconds, then Roy smacked the desk with his open hand.

"Why did this have to happen today?" He whirled around and started toward the door, then looked back at me. He seemed so fierce I was afraid to say anything. He flung his arms out dramatically.

"Don't you see how hard it will be for me to preach tomorrow, knowing this?" He groaned. "My first opportunity for months!" He screwed up his lips and jammed his hands deep into his pockets.

"I don't know whether to call the police or what."

"Oh, no!" I touched my throat and gasped. "No! We mustn't do anything until Richard comes back. It wouldn't be fair—"

"Are you *still* protecting him?" Roy's mouth drew down sarcastically. "What's it going to take, Louise?"

I couldn't answer. I bit my lip and was conscious of turning my ring around and around. Roy picked up the steno pad.

"At least I'd better take care of this. The police will want it." His face and attitude reminded me of a soldier. Suddenly his features softened and he touched my shoulder.

"Do you see why I wanted you to get away? Don't you think it would be better for you to go back to Portland and not get involved?" He tipped my chin up and looked into my eyes. "It will be hard on your reputation if things get, well— messy."

I jerked my face away and looked out the window.

"I can't go home, at least not right away." I looked back

at Roy. "My aunt recently got married. There's no place for me."

"No kidding—well, I just don't want you to get hurt." He took a deep breath. "So. Let's both try to pretend everything is the same. When is Richard due back?"

"Probably around 6:00 tomorrow night."

"All right. Let's plan to meet with him right after church tomorrow night. Meanwhile, I'll put this notebook in a safe place."

"It's safe enough in my desk drawer," I protested.

"Oh, no. When you tell Richard what we want to talk about, he might destroy the evidence before we could do anything."

"Oh, Roy, I think we're both over-reacting. I wish I hadn't told you." I tried to look aloof and calm, but my heart was racing and my hands were cold.

"I hope we are over-reacting," he said softly. He took three steps and was out the door. I was alone with my thoughts which were not making any sense. I reached up to pat my hair and was dismayed when I realized Roy had seen me with my hair in curlers. But so what? I thought. He no longer appealed to me. I wasn't sure I even liked him.

And Richard? What of my love for him? I put my head down on my arms and felt the hot tears well up. This was a nightmare! The heat and the silence seemed to close in, smothering me.

I stood up, slammed the desk drawer shut and hurried out. I would go to my room and rest. I hadn't had much sleep in the last twenty-four hours. I probably was hungry, too. I would go to get something to eat, then go to my room and rest. And pray.

I was awake, but I thought I was dreaming. The tower chimes were ringing just as they had that other night. I rolled out of bed, yanked on blue jeans and a tee shirt, and rammed my feet into tennis shoes. The tongue on the left shoe went down inside and I was conscious of it being uncomfortable, but there was no time to take it off and fix it because I had to stop the chimes. Richard wasn't here, Esther probably had her ear plugs in, and Harry had a reputation for being able to sleep through an earthquake. It was up to me to get up to the tower room and disconnect the timer. Dickie came in through the bathroom door just as I had dumped everything out of my purse, trying to find the church keys.

"The chimes are ringing!" he shouted.

"Yes, honey, I know. I'm going over there right now. Get back to bed."

I ran down the stairs and out the back door. It would be quicker to go through the front, but I had never unlocked the big church doors and I didn't want to try to learn now.

The playground was almost completely black, and I couldn't take time to run back for my flashlight. What a dumb time for the outside lights to be off! Something must have gone wrong with those timers, too.

After a little fumbling, I unlocked the school door and heard it slam behind me as I felt along the wall for the light switch. The light was reassuring, but the deafening clanging of the chimes made me frantic. I ran down the hall, past the carpeted portion, turned left into the narthex and found myself in darkness again. I couldn't remember where the switch panel was, but I finally found it. I flipped on the light in the baptistry, then in the choir loft and sanctuary before the narthex lit up.

My heart was beating hard and my hands were shaking as I put the little key in the lock and opened the door to the tower. I flipped the light switch, but no light came on. I flipped it back and forth and moaned. It had to come on. But it didn't. The bulb must have burned out.

Some light from the narthex filtered in on the stairway, and I hoped there might be some light coming in through the louvres from the street lights in front. I *had* to shut that mechanism off, whether there was light or not, so I climbed blindly up the stairs.

After I passed the first landing I was in complete darkness. I was terrified. I began to creep up the stairs, feeling my way and dreading each step. The higher I climbed, the thicker the darkness became. It was like black wool, hot and suffocating. The darkness and the jarring chimes reminded me of a haunted house I had once visited on Halloween, but *that* night I knew I was safe and it was fun to be scared. All I could think of now was the terror of being locked in—or something worse.

After several moments of deafening, ear-shattering chimes-clanging, I finally found the recorder. My fingers searched out the timer and switched it off. I turned around and could now make out a dim, grey square which was the stairwell. I held my keys tightly and started for the stairs. At least I knew I wouldn't be locked in this time.

There was no warning. A hand clamped across my mouth and my arms were fastened to my sides. It felt as though I was in the arms of a giant. One finger was across my nostrils and I couldn't breathe. I kicked, twisted, bowed my back and tried to bite, but I was caught. Insanely, I thought this must be the way poor calves feel when they're roped and tied.

I sucked in with all my might trying to get a little air. My head pounded and I knew I was going to die soon. I quit fighting and a voice whispered in my ear, "Curiousity killed the cat."

17

I could hear voices but the words meant nothing. Someone kept touching my head, pushing it. It hurt. I seemed to be in a group of ten people, riding in an open car on rails, and we were hurtling down a straight track at tremendous speed. Multicolored lights whizzed by. I hung on to the side of the car and struggled with someone. I wanted to stay in the car, but a person in authority said, "You cannot stay here. You must leap into the nine group."

I had to go. They pulled and pushed at me until I was forced into the next car and I became a "nine." I liked it after I got there, and wanted to stay, but another stern voice said, "Now you must jump into the eight car."

I screamed and pulled back, but they made me go; then I became a "seven." Shortly, I was forced into the "sixes." Oh, Father, won't it ever end? I was pushed to the "fives," then "fours," and then the "threes." At last, there were only two of us. Of course, I reasoned, I had died and was with the Lord.

"Would you like for me to sing?" I asked Him, and opened my eyes.

A sweet-faced lady in a green cap and uniform was beside me.

"I'd love to hear you sing." She smiled at me and I realized I was in a hospital. My head ached and I was sick.

I slept.

Later, Dr. Fowler came into the room. He stood beside the bed and shook his head at me as though I were a naughty child.

"How long have I been here?" I asked. It hurt my lips to talk.

"Well, little girl, the rescue squad brought you in about one-thirty Sunday morning, and this is Monday morning."

My first thought was that I had missed Roy's sermon. I tried to sit up, but Doc held me down. The movement hurt my back and legs and I discovered my left arm was bandaged from the wrist to the elbow. Dr. Fowler smiled.

"Do you remember falling down the stairs?"

I gasped.

"I didn't fall down the stairs!"

"Sure you did. And you came within an ace of killing yourself. I don't know what I'm going to do with you if you don't quit running around in the dark." He studied my chart for a moment. "You'll remember everything in a day or two."

I felt frantic, and reached out to pull his sleeve.

"Dr. Fowler, I did not fall! I've got to get out of here." My voice sounded strange to me, as though I had a band across my throat.

He shook his head again and frowned. "You're not going anywhere for about a week." His face softened then and he winked, "See you tonight." He was gone.

If my head hadn't ached so badly I might have had presence of mind enough to detain him, and try to learn who found me and if they had caught the person who had attacked me. I raised my head just enough to see myself in the mirror across the room. I couldn't believe what I saw. My head was almost completely wrapped in bandages, there was a big white patch on my chin, and one eye was almost swollen shut. My lips looked puffy, too. The effort to sit up hurt me all over and I dropped back on the pillow. I touched my rib cage gingerly and discovered wide bands of tape. Unshed tears began to sting my eyes, but I willed myself not to cry. Every movement, whether internal or external, hurt. I closed my eyes, too weary and in too much pain to even pray.

"Louise?" a familiar voice whispered, and I opened my eyes. Richard was standing in the doorway.

"Richard—" I moved my fingers and he came swiftly to the bed and took my hand. His hand felt hard and warm and I couldn't keep the tears from my eyes. I felt my mouth turn down and tremble and my throat ached. He sat down in a chair and scooted it close to me. He stroked my forehead and cheeks. His face looked tense, his eyes dark with concern. Neither of us spoke. We were still for a minute or two, then I spoke through swollen lips.

"Did they tell you what happened?"

"Yes. Dickie and I got to you about the same time."

I stared at him.

"What do you mean? Weren't you in the mountains?"

"I came home Saturday night." He looked at me and then away.

"But you weren't supposed to be home until Sunday afternoon."

"I came home early," he explained, "because I got food poisoning, along with several others."

"Oh, my darling! Oh, Richard, I'm so sorry." I tried to squeeze his hand, but my fingers didn't grip very tightly.

"Don't worry," he said putting his face near mine. "I wasn't very sick." He smiled one-sidedly. "I only threw up once."

"Ooh, sick," I said.

"But some of the men were really sick," he continued, "so they decided to call off the retreat." He leaned back in the chair, but kept holding my hand. "When I drove up in the parking lot Saturday night I saw the lights on in the church and thought Harry had forgotten to turn them out. When I came through the front door, Dickie was just coming down the hall."

I took a deep breath, and he looked at me anxiously.

"Is this too tiring?"

"Oh, no!" I protested. "I have to know whom you saw."

"Saw?" He tipped his head to one side. "All we saw was you, crumpled up on the bottom step of the tower room."

Although my head ached with each beat of my heart, my brain had grasped the fact that Richard had been at church Saturday night. Vera's suicide note plus the other notes flashed into my mind. I seemed to hear Roy's accusations against Richard. Had he come home earlier than he said? Had he somehow heard Roy and me talking, decided to lure me to the bell tower and silence me—(as perhaps Vera had been silenced)? The expression on Richard's face this moment was compassionate, but he could be faking it.

I thought of the hand that had covered my nose and mouth, and terror began to well up inside of me. It would be easy for him to smother me right here in this bed. My breath began to come faster and my eyes widened as I watched Richard lean toward me.

"Louise! What is it? Are you in terrible pain?"

Maybe it was the pain or the medication, but all the doubts I had about Richard began to pile up in my throat and came out in a scream. The sound was thin and pitiful, as a scream is in a nightmare. Richard tried to comfort me but I twisted and turned and screamed again and again. He put his hand over my mouth and I lost consciousness.

When I came to, I heard Richard say, "I don't know what's wrong with her. We were talking and suddenly she seemed to be horrified. That's when she fainted." I opened my good eye just enough to see a nurse standing beside me, taking my pulse. (Thank you, Father, for letting the nurse hear me scream.)

She made a note on my chart and said, "She'll be all right, Reverend. But maybe you should go now. I'll call Dr. Fowler and tell him."

Just as I had finished a dinner of thick, tasteless soup and red gelatin dessert, Dr. Fowler swung jauntily into the room. He glanced at the other bed, now curtained.

"See you have a roomie tonight. Good. Keep you from being

lonesome.''

"She's just three years older than I am," I whispered, "and she already has two children."

"Now, see? If you behave yourself and quit running around in the dark and getting your head split open, maybe some nice man will marry you and I can deliver babies for you instead of patching you up." I thought of Richard, the man I had wanted to marry. An involuntary shudder went through me.

"Dr. Fowler, it will be visiting hours pretty soon, won't it?" He looked at his watch.

"About thirty-five minutes. Why?"

"Can I request no visitors?"

He looked at me from under his brows in a searching way. "No visitors? Why is that?"

I knew it must seem strange to him. Most patients want visitors, but I wasn't ready to explain to Dr. Fowler about my fears and suspicions. Nothing was really clear to me, except there had been an attempt on my life. If I talked to anyone else, I decided, it would be the police. But just as it was the night I was attacked on the playground, I had no evidence. I wasn't ready to talk to the police, either. If only I had a friend! Someone I could talk it out with, someone who would help me.

For the first time I thought of Esther. I could talk to her. But what about Harry? If I told her everything, it would implicate him. I could tell her almost everything and leave out the part about seeing him and his camper. I could at least talk to her about the suicide note.

"I guess the reason I don't want visitors just yet is because of how I acted today when the pastor came to see me," I said. "I began to cry while he was here. I'm sure the nurse told you."

He nodded.

"That's a fairly normal reaction after what you've been through. Now don't get a complex about it. You need some company."

"The only person I want to see right now is Esther." I looked at him as sternly as I could with one eye and swollen lips. "Will you tell them at the desk?"

"All right, missy. But it won't be long until you'll be wishing you had some company.''

Dr. Fowler must have called Esther, because at exactly
7:00 o'clock she peeked in the door. She couldn't hide her
distress at seeing me and tears came to her eyes. She rushed
to me and her wrinkled face seemed to crumple even more. She
perched on the edge of the chair by my bed.

"Oh, ya l'il darlin','' she moaned. "Ya poor, poor, l'il thing.''
She leaned toward me and touched my arm.

It was comforting to have her make over me and I felt tears
come to my eyes. In the short time I had known her, I had
learned to respect and love her. She seemed more like my
mother all the time.

"Oh, Esther,'' I sobbed, "It's been so awful!''

"There, there, sweet baby,'' she cooed. "Honey, how on
earth could ya get so bunged up?''

"Esther, I've got to talk to you. I've got to tell you some
things before something else happens to me.'' I was whisper-
ing so my roommate and her husband wouldn't hear.

"I believe someone is trying to kill me!'' She looked at me
as though I had a high fever and was out of my head.

"Well, honey, anybody can see ya've been hurt, but—''

I grabbed her big, bony wrist and held it as hard as I could.

"Please listen to me!'' Esther's eyes widened with shock and
the girl in the next bed looked over at me. I lowered my voice
to a whisper again.

"Esther, do you care for me?''

"Why, honey! Ya know I do,'' she answered in a throaty
whisper.

"Then listen, and don't interrupt because I may not have
another chance to tell you.'' Her head bobbed up and down
and her eyes looked extra wide behind her thick glasses. At
last I knew she would listen.

"When I first came to work,'' I began, "about a month
after I started, Roy—Mr. Decker—told me he thought the pastor
had stolen a hundred dollars—''

"A hundred dollars?''

"Didn't you know that a hundred dollars had been stolen
from the floor safe?''

"No, I didn't,'' she said hoarsely, "nobody tells me nothin'.

But I'd be willing to stake my life the pastor didn't steal no hundred dollars!''

"Sh-h!" I warned. "That's exactly how I felt, and I told Mr. Decker so. Then he told me that there were many in the church who felt that he not only took the money, but that he was the reason Vera took her life!''

Esther clapped her hand over her mouth and her shaggy eyebrows peaked in alarm. Slowly she took her hand away and whispered, "That's Satan talking. Them two loved each other. I don't know why she killed herself, but it didn't have nothin' to do with 'im.''

I wanted to believe her. With all my heart I wanted Richard to be the man I thought he was. I beckoned for her to lean close and continued in a barely audible whisper.

"Then, Shirley Bennett—you know, the teacher? Where I was this weekend?" Esther nodded. "She said she believed it was the pastor's fault, too, that he had stolen the money, and that the congregation wasn't going to call him again this fall. She even intimated that maybe the pastor and Vanessa Hamilton were..." I looked at Esther. We had never discussed anything that bordered on sex, but she knew what I was talking about.

Her eyes narrowed and her wrinkled, brown face took on a fierce look. "I've jest never heard so many lies.''

"I felt that way, too, and I told both of them, Shirley and Roy. Oh, yes! Beverly Wrightwood, the secretary, feels the same way as they do.''

"Why, Mrs. Wrightwood and Vera was the best a friends.''

"I know. Anyhow, I told all three of them that although I didn't know the pastor very well, I respected him and, as far as I could see, both at the office and at home, he was a good man. And—I told them I was going to try to find out who did take the money so I could clear his name.''

"Bless ya, honey.''

"It was right after that when I got locked in the bell tower. Do you remember? Harry let me out that day, and we all sort of called it a 'strange thing.' But later, Richard told me he thought someone *had* locked me in." Esther's eyes were large and fearful. Suddenly, I was exhausted. I breathed deeply and rested for a moment.

"Oh, Esther, there are so many things to tell you." I shook my head slowly on the pillow. "That day before Harry let me out of the tower room, I found a little cartoon drawing on a scrap of paper. It was like a child had drawn it, and it was a picture of a dead cat!" I shuddered.

"What on earth!"

"And another thing I just remember," I went on, "Vanessa Hamilton has made some ugly, threatening remarks to me."

"Ya don't say!" All of Esther's "s's" made a whistling noise.

"When I told her I was doing everything I could to clear up the pastor's name, she told me to be careful or I might find myself in a big city without a job."

"Why, honey, I can't understand why she would talk to ya like that." Suddenly her eyes opened even wider and so did her mouth. "Oh, oh! I jest remembered it was Mrs. Hamilton who wanted to know where the pastor was that night of the VBS dinner. She was the one who wouldn't listen to me when I was goin' to explain where ya two were."

Bits and pieces began to fit together and started to flash through my mind like a home movie on fast rewind. Vanessa was as tall as I, in perfect physical condition. Could she have been the one who attacked me in the tower? She would have had the advantage. But did she have a key? And did she know how to set off the mechanism?

I recalled her threat to me to leave the pastor alone. If she believed I had gone some place with him for the weekend—but then, how would she know I had come back?

My insides began to shake uncontrollably. How could I, a plain, peace-loving dummy be in such trouble? Not just trouble—danger. I had to finish telling Esther. At least if I was killed, she would be able to tell the police.

"Well, Vanessa Hamilton also told me—" I bit my lip. "Esther, I don't want you to be shocked, but I've got to tell you these things."

"'Course, honey, ya go ahead."

"She told me to keep away from Richard, because she intended to marry him!" Esther's mouth dropped open again.

"So, I'm sure she wouldn't do anything to hurt his reputation. I don't know who took the money."

Off to one side of my mind, I suddenly realized that if Vera had been murdered, possibly Vanessa had a motive. But I didn't want to get ahead of myself, so I continued, "So far I haven't uncovered anything. I only know somebody wants me to quit trying."

"Now, honey—"

"Remember that night you had such a bad headache? Well, that night I saw lights out in the storeroom, so I went out there. There were—" I hesitated because I didn't want to name Harry—"there were two men in the storeroom and they seemed to be unloading TV's, cameras, stereos—stuff like that."

Esther rubbed the side of her face. Her mouth was still open and I could tell by her dubious expression she was having trouble believing all of these things. I didn't blame her because I could hardly believe it myself.

"Somehow they discovered me and somebody hit me on top of the head." Esther started to speak, but I hurried on.

"I know what you're going to say, Esther. Harry was the one who found me, and he and Richard and Dr. Fowler all said I stumbled over my own feet and fell on my head!" I knew a little sarcasm had crept into my voice. "Don't you see, Esther? I *know* I didn't fall down!"

She looked so worried and miserable I felt sorry for her. She licked her lower lip and spoke hesitantly.

"Did ya ever tell Pastor all this?"

"Yes." I thought of that day when he had kissed me. I had been so in love. Now I was afraid of him.

"I told him the whole thing, and he agreed that it certainly seemed that some of the people thought he was guilty, and that someone was trying to get me to quit defending him."

There was a gentle stirring in the next bed and my roommate said goodbye to her husband. He stood up, nodded politely to us and left the room.

"It's eight o'clock, Esther. You'd better go. But just one more thing. Do you, by any chance, know the exact time Richard came home Saturday night?"

"No, honey, I don't. I did wake up that night, though. I

150

looked at my clock and it was just after midnight, and I got wide awake 'cause Harry wasn't home yet.'' She looked down at her hands.

"He'd gone to see some old war buddy and I always worry a little he might start drinkin' agin.'' She looked up and smiled. "It's been seven years now since he's had a drink. Ya know, honey, he's never gone forward to confess Christ in public, but I know he's a believer in his heart.''

Harry wasn't with Esther Saturday night! I had always distrusted him and knew he was doing something dishonest, but I couldn't figure out a motive for him to undermine the pastor or hurt me. I was sure his apparent friendship and respect for the pastor was genuine and, if he didn't like the pastor, he and Esther would simply move on. Still, he could have been the one who hit me that night on the playground.

My head ached and I couldn't stand to think about it any longer, but my brain wouldn't quit. Esther leaned over and kissed me. I looked up at her.

"Do you believe me?'' My voice sounded babyish.

"Yes, honey, I know ya wouldn't lie to me. Sure is awful goings on for church folks, though.''

"Don't tell anybody what I've told you tonight, not even Harry. Promise me.'' She nodded her head. "Because I've got to find out who's trying to get me. I don't want to accuse anybody—and I don't want to lose my job.''

She stood over me and love seemed to flow out of her eyes to me.

"Child, ya go to sleep.''

The hospital room looked strange in the semi-dark. I looked over at the next bed and wondered if the girl was asleep. We had both been given sedatives and I was beginning to feel drowsy but I fought it. I felt that if I went to sleep, I would never wake up.

18

I was permitted to leave the hospital Wednesday morning.

Richard came for me and, although I was slightly apprehensive, it was wonderful to ride with him again. The three days in the hospital had given me time to think about every facet of my accidents, and I had about come to the conclusion that, even though Richard had been present at every one of my "catastrophes," there was just too much in his favor to ever seriously consider him capable of hurting me. On Monday and Tuesday he had simply ignored my request for no visitors and come to see me anyway.

"Pastors can come anytime," he explained to me, and winked. He brought me carnations, sat with me during every visiting hour, and read to me. Sometimes I would catch him looking at my bruised face with tears in his eyes. He would lean over and gently touch my cheek. As unbelievable as it seemed, I began to believe he loved me—or else he was putting on the greatest act in the world.

Both of us were quiet as we rode along. I had so many things I wanted to say and also many questions. I glanced over at him just as he looked at me and we both smiled.

"Forgive me, Richard, for telling Dr. Fowler I didn't want you to visit me." He shrugged.

"I knew you'd been through a terrible time," he said. "I didn't blame you."

"I don't know what made me think you would hurt me, but when you put your hand over my mouth, I remembered how I had almost smothered—"

He reached out to comfort me, but my left arm was still bandaged. His hand hovered for a moment, then he put it back on the steering wheel.

"I shouldn't have put my hand on your mouth that night," he agreed, "but I guess I panicked too, with you screaming and fighting me. I was afraid you were going to hurt yourself ."

I smiled and nodded my head.

"Try to forget all that now, Louise. When frightening thoughts come to your mind, quote Scripture."

"I read the Bible quite a bit in the hospital, but my good eye tired easily." He flashed a smile at me.

"Excuses, excuses," he mocked. I was happy and in love again.

"How's Dickie?" I asked.

"Ornery as ever. He thinks he's pretty important since he helped find you. I think he's fallen in love with you."

I laughed with pleasure.

"I know! He sent me the cutest letter."

"He asked me if I wouldn't try to figure out a way to have you be his mom."

I could feel my face get red. *Oh, Dickie, I'd love to be your mom.* I flicked a glance at Richard.

"So what did you say?" I asked.

We stopped for a red light and Richard turned to look at me. His dark eyes were soft; he drew a quick breath.

"I told him I'd see what I could do."

My heart did the elevator ride sensation again. Was that a proposal? I wanted to slide over close to him, but instead I stared straight ahead and waited for my heart to start beating normally again. After the light turned green and we started moving, I changed the subject.

"Did you hear Roy preach Sunday?"

"Yes, I did. It was a fine sermon."

"I'm sorry I didn't get to hear him. Did you tell him about me?"

"Yes, but Louise, I didn't tell him you were attacked. Everyone thinks you fell down the stairs."

I nodded. He had told me in the hospital that unless I insisted, the police wouldn't be notified.

"Something like that could really hurt the church," he said.

"But remember, Richard, somebody wants me out of the way." I looked at him. "Sometimes I don't think you believe me, either."

"I do believe you, Louise, but it's hard for me to point a finger at any of our people." He turned into the church driveway and parked the station wagon. It was going to be a hot day and it was already hot in the car, but Richard settled back and turned to look at me. He put his arm along the back of the seat and reached out for a strand of my hair.

"The people are already split on their opinion of me," he said. "That in itself isn't important, except that it affects the work." His hand dropped so his fingers touched my shoulder.

"I really believe that if I can hang on, keep on keeping on, in time they will forget Vera's tragedy and we can concentrate on the task the Lord has given us of winning this neighborhood to Christ."

I nodded agreement, but I was thinking how beautiful his eyes were.

He took his arm away and started to get out of the car.

"The general feeling is better, I believe," he went on, "but if we have to bring in the police and have an investigation, it may undo everything." He opened his door.

"But, Louise, I don't want you to think I am glossing over what's happened to you. I just want us to be sure before we call in the police."

"But, Richard, what shall I do?" I couldn't bear the thought of being physically hurt again. "Maybe it would be better if I went back to Portland."

"Oh, no!" he said as he came around to my side. He was grinning when he opened my door. "I'm not about to break in another secretary!" When I got out of the car I felt light-headed and was glad he held me in a strong grip all the way across the lawns.

He eased me down on the couch in the parsonage. "The first thing we're going to do is play detective." He sat close to me. "We'll go over every detail and, when we've decided who our enemy is, we'll set a trap."

I looked at him to see if he was joking, but his face was grim.

"Meanwhile, you aren't going to be out of my sight." He leaned toward me and I closed my eyes. But before he could kiss me, Esther clumped into the room.

"There's my children!" She rushed to me and I was caught up in a perfumy, motherly hug.

"Why, ya look so much better! Your eye is pert near open." She gave me another squeeze and I winced. My body was still sore all over.

"Pastor, I've got an important message for ya." She reached into her apron pocket and read from a square of paper. "A Mrs. Doheney lives in Bakersfield, and her husband is dying. Here's the phone number."

Richard read the message for himself, then said, "Why,

154

that's Barbara Doheney, remember her Esther? She and her children were members here about four years ago, and then her husband was transferred." He stood up. "I'll call right now."

Esther made over me some more and told me a cute thing Dickie had said. In a few minutes Richard was back, with a worried look on his face.

"Well, there's nothing I can do but go to Bakersfield." He sighed deeply. "Barbara says Mack is dying of cancer, and he's never received Christ. She says she knows if I come and talk to him, he will."

"Oh, Richard! I don't want you to go!"

"My darling, I don't want to go, either—and I don't think anything I can say at this point will change him, but she seems so certain, and the kids want me to come, too." He looked at his watch.

"I can be there by 2:30 or 3:00 this afternoon, and maybe I won't have to spend the night." His face brightened a little. "We never know how the Lord will work. This might be the time Mack will become a Christian."

He went to his room and in about five minutes he came back with his shaving kit in one hand and a coat on a hanger, hooked on a finger of his other hand. He put the things down on the couch beside me, then helped me to my feet.

"Now, I'm going to help you up to your bed, and you are not to leave that room until I come back, understand?" He tried to look stern but his features were softened by a touch of love.

"Esther, you're my witness. Take her meals to her and don't let her come down. And don't let anyone in to see her—except Dickie." Esther and I both looked at him. "I mean it," he said harshly. "I'll tell Roy to take care of things while I'm gone. Now come on, little girl, up those stairs."

The next morning I couldn't get over how much better I felt. I looked better, too, I noticed, as I dressed and combed my hair.

Richard had told me to stay in my room, but I decided I had to go to work. The bulletin couldn't wait, and there were dozens of other things that should be done.

It hurt to walk down the stairs, and I took them one step at a time. But when I walked into the kitchen I made myself move lightly, without limping.

Harry was sitting at the table when I got there. He looked up and forced a smile. He wasn't glad to see me and I wondered why. Well, I wasn't especially glad to see him either. Even though Richard had said he seemed like a good old boy, I was suspicious of him. I didn't know what he was involved in, but I knew it couldn't be right.

"How are you, Harry?" I asked politely.

"Me?" He yawned noisily and stretched. "I'm okay. How about you? You're not s'posed to be up yet, are you?"

"No, but I know there's a lot of work on my desk, and I really feel good, so I'm going over this morning." I went to the refrigerator and took out a container of orange juice.

"Where's Esther?"

"Oh, them folks next door invited her and Dickie to go down to the beach today."

"Really? She didn't say a word about it last night."

"She may not have known about it. In fact, I don't think she did 'cause she and Dickie were rushing around getting their beach duds together this morning."

He got up and poured himself another cup of coffee. Although his shirt looked clean, I could smell his odor as he moved around. I had intended to make a piece of toast, but my appetite had vanished. He sat down again and I took the chair opposite him.

"She told me she'd rather not go to the beach," he continued, "but Dickie wanted to go so bad, and it was the first time they'd ever invited her. She didn't want to leave you, but I told her I'd see to it you behaved yourself."

He smiled then, and seemed a little more relaxed. I looked at him carefully. His eyes were too small for his face and were bloodshot, but the expression in them was warm and friendly. Was he a friend?

A stranger might describe him as a middle-aged, fat and jolly person, who loved children, a kind, grandfatherly type. But he had been the one who let me out of the tower the first time, and he was the one who had found me on the playground

156

the second time. But if it was Harry who had stolen the money and attacked me, what did he have to gain by discrediting the pastor or hurting me? Roy had mentioned several times how penny-pinching Richard was. Maybe Harry felt if there was a different preacher he'd get a larger salary.

Without considering the consequences I said, "Harry, you know that night on the playground?" His smile faded and he nodded. "I saw you and another man in the store room."

He looked at me and his mouth opened. He leaned forward and rubbed his mouth and chin with a grimy hand. His face lost some of its color.

"I was afraid of that," he said.

There was a staccato knock at the back screen.

"Howdy!" It was Roy. "Anybody home?"

"Sure!" Harry called. To me he whispered, "Don't tell Esther. I'll explain later." He got up and met Roy as he came in. "Want a cup of coffee, Mr. Decker?"

"Don't mind if I—Louise! What are you doing out of bed?"

"I'm practically well," I smiled and curtseyed to cover how upset I was. What had made me tell Harry?

"Are you sure? You don't want to have a relapse."

"Relapse? I won't have a relapse. I haven't had the flu."

"Just the same, Doc Fowler said you almost killed yourself the other night. If you move around too much, you might start something bleeding."

I wrinkled my nose in disdain. "I'm going to work this morning."

He shook his head, helpless to do anything with me.

"Does Esther know about this?"

Harry explained where Esther was and then Roy turned to me.

"If you're really well enough to come to the office, I'd appreciate it. Richard asked me to cover for him but he said he hoped to get back last night.

"I'm coming right now," I said. It hurt to stand up, but I smiled confidently.

Harry stood up and stretched again. He beamed a special look at me, then said, "Well, guess I'd better get going, too. Got to get the crab grass out of the rose beds today."

From my office window, I could see many gorgeous rose-buds. I took the scissors from my drawer and went out the front way to cut several. I put water in a vase, placed the arrangement on my desk, then sat down and began to open the mail. I wondered if Roy had said anything to Richard about the notes.

At coffee break time I would go into his office and ask him. I looked at my watch. It was too early for a coffee break, but maybe I would go anyway. Before I had a chance to get up, Roy appeared in the doorway, smiling as usual, with a cup of coffee in his hand. I was a little frustrated because I hadn't really decided what to say.

"What can I do for you, Mr. Decker?" I said, bantering.

"No work, Louise, so you can relax." He grinned charmingly. "No, I was just curious to know if you said anything to Richard about the suicide notes."

"Isn't that interesting! I was just going to come in to your office and ask you the same thing! No—I haven't said anything about the notes because what we were thinking will hurt him."

Roy jerked his head back and rolled his eyes up.

"Hurt him! Good grief, girl, I thought you'd learned your lesson about playing protector for him." He shook his head, obviously disgusted. How could I tell him I not only wanted to protect Richard, but that I was also in love with him?

"Roy, I know you think he took that money, and also caused Vera's death, but I talked to Esther while I was in the hospital, and I'm convinced Richard loved Vera."

"You talked to Esther?" He put his cup down on my desk and sat down in the nearest chair.

"Well, *you* were thinking about calling the police," I said defensively.

"Not any more," he said. "I've decided the police must not be called in."

"No matter who?"

"No, the police will just cause a big scandal and we'll lose church members and students." He looked at me with his unblinking, protruding eyes. "We have to think of the future, Louise."

His whole attitude was earnest and sincere.

"I'm hoping when Richard is confronted with the evidence of those notes, he'll have the decency to resign."

"Wait a minute, Roy. I think we've been wrong. I've changed my mind since I've been in the hospital. I am positive it couldn't have been Richard." His eyes narrowed.

"Who, then?"

"I don't know." I shuffled some papers on my desk.

"Have you thought about Harry?"

"What about Harry?" Roy sucked in a mouthful of coffee.

"Harry and Esther aren't rich, you know, and I'll bet Harry has a key to the safe." Roy stuck out his lips and shook his head.

"Nope. We found that out when the money was stolen."

"Did anybody actually check that big ring of keys?"

Roy stared at me and blinked his eyes. I felt encouraged. At least he seemed to be considering someone besides Richard. "He also has keys to this office," I continued. "He can come and go as he pleases."

I wondered if I should tell Roy about that night on the playground. As usual, my mouth took over before my brain could do anything and I blurted, "Roy, that night on the playground, when I fell, I saw Harry and some other man in the storeroom."

All sounds and movement seemed to stop and I could hear Roy breathing. At last, he sat up straighter and looked at me.

"Who was the other man?"

"I don't know."

"Would you know him again?"

"I doubt it. I only saw his back, and I got the impression he had sort of long, curly hair. Dark, I think."

"What were they doing?"

"They seemed to be looking at equipment, or hauling it in or out. I saw a camera and some stereo equipment, I think, and there was a TV in the camper—"

"In the camper?"

"Yes; see I had sneaked around to the back and there was Harry's camper, with the door open—"

Roy shook his head from side to side and grinned in disbelief.

"You are a nosy little thing, aren't you?" He stood up and

patted the top of my head. "How about a cup of coffee?" He picked up his cup and started toward the door. "Stay put. I'll be right back. I've got to know what other wonders you've seen." He chuckled slightly and shook his head again. "What a snoopy."

I had only opened one letter when he was back with two steaming cups of coffee. When he put them down, I noticed a bulge in his coat pocket.

"I really need this coffee," I said, as I picked up the mug. Although it was going to be another hot day, it was almost cold in the office now and the heat felt good on my hands. I sipped it and scalded my tongue.

Roy sat down and looked at me expectantly.

"All right, now tell me what else you've uncovered." He smiled at me and for a moment I remembered how infatuated I had been with him. He was good-looking and had so much personality.

I took another swallow of coffee and said dramatically, "Now let me see." I put my finger to my head and I suddenly felt dizzy. Maybe it *was* too soon for me to be at work. I blinked my eyes and shook my head slightly.

"What's wrong?" Roy asked.

"I don't know. I feel sort of light-headed." I swallowed hard and opened my eyes as wide as I could.

"Drink the rest of your coffee. That will brace you."

Roy stood up and his face looked very white and large as he loomed over me. I saw him reach into his coat pocket and take out a roll of mailing tape, the kind that has strands of nylon running through it. What a strange thing to do, I thought, but said nothing. I was having difficulty sitting in my chair. I kept wanting to lie down and go to sleep.

"Hold out your hands, Louise." Roy said and zipped off a long piece of tape, reached over for my scissors and cut if off. Meekly, I held out my hands. I thought he was going to help me stand up, but before I could comprehend what he was doing, he had wrapped the tape around my wrists tightly and I was handcuffed.

"You're hurting my left arm!" I wanted to say, but couldn't utter a sound. I watched mutely as he cut off another piece and placed it firmly across my mouth. I made a feeble effort to stand, but my legs were dead.

19

With all my will, I tried to stand up. I knew Roy had drugged me and, although my thoughts seemed to be wrapped in cotton, I also knew that Roy had been the one in the tower and that now he would finish what he had started.

"Don't struggle, Louise." He smiled at me as a parent smiles at a child who is about to get vaccinated. "Actually, it's quite merciful of me to give you the sedative. Otherwise, you would suffer a great deal." He walked over to the door and locked it.

"By the way," he grinned broadly, "I, too, have a key to the safe!" He took out his key case, selected a thin key about two inches long and held it up.

Roy seemed to waver as I looked at him, as a television screen when the horizontal control needs to be adjusted. "I thought you'd like to know the answers, before—well, I tried to warn you, 'Curiosity killed the cat,' remember?" He laughed in his throat and kissed the key.

"Ah, Louise, Louise! When I came to work here three years ago, your dear Richard loaned me his keys one afternoon so I could have access to his library. Wasn't that decent of him?"

I could barely hold my eyes open, but I kept biting on my tongue until I could feel the pain, and digging my fingernails into my palms in an effort to stay awake.

"Naturally, I didn't waste time that afternoon looking at dry, spiritual tomes." He giggled like a little boy.

"I scooted over to the hardware store and had keys made! I didn't know what they were for, but I was sure someday I'd need them! Wasn't that ingenious?" He came close to me and went down on one knee.

"See, Louise, what a clever man you've rejected?" He took a shock of my hair, twisted it tightly and pulled my head back. "And you did reject me, Louise! Don't you think I know what you said to Richard?" He pointed to the air vent near the ceiling.

"I can hear every word up in the sixth grade room." He stood up, put one hand on his hip and sauntered around the room.

" 'I think I'm in love with you, Richard' " he mimicked in a high-pitched voice. "Fool!" He walked over to the wall and picked up the frayed typewriter cord and examined it.

"This will do nicely." He turned to face me. "Why did you have to reject me, Louise? I didn't think *you* would. But, you're just like all of them. Just like Vera, too."

I tried to get up, but I seemed almost paralyzed.

"Oh, that startles you, does it?" His eyes half closed, he put his hands in his pockets and rocked back and forth.

"She sat there, just as you are, and told me she had seen me unlock the safe." He flicked his tongue over his lips.

"Don't you see? I couldn't let her ruin the plan. I had figured it out so carefully. Nobody knew I had a key to the safe, and everyone would have to think Richard took the money. Wasn't a hundred dollars a clever amount to take?"

He seemed to be floating in the room like some weird ectoplasm.

"I could have used more than the hundred, but I wanted it to be a petty amount, enough to be important, but not too much, you see." He clapped his hands and laughed.

"And it worked, too! Almost everyone thinks he took it, or at least they wonder. But Vera would have told on me." He stuck out his lip in a little-boy pout. "So I gave *her* some coffee." He grinned sadistically and, in my drugged state, his teeth looked like toadstools in a watermelon mouth.

"I didn't give her as much as I gave you, because I just wanted her to feel sick. Then I could help her home, and finish her off in her own bedroom—but no, she insisted she had to call on some of her Sunday School pupils that day. So, I helped her over to the garage. That's when I got the idea of carbon monoxide poisoning. Sheer luck! And the note was sheer luck." He snickered and clapped his hands again.

"After I got the hose rigged up and she was unconscious, I came back here to see if I'd left any evidence. That's when I found the ready-made suicide note." He floated back into my vision.

"But I didn't know about those other notes until you showed them to me. That's when I knew I was going to have to get rid of you. I was afraid from the start you were going to cause me trouble, and I tried to scare you away, but you don't scare. I tried to warn you, Louise. Weren't my cat drawings cute? You should have gone back to Portland, and then you would have been safe." He came to me and put his hands gently on my face.

"Dear Louise. I didn't want to hurt you, but to be frank, you're just plain nosy. Don't you see?"

He was going around the room now, scratching his head and then rubbing his shoulders.

"If you drove a car, I could have had another monoxide suicide—monoxide suicide! It has a nice rhythm, yes? But, now I'll have to rig up an electrocution." He rubbed his hands together.

"It won't be too hard. I'll just roll your chair back and forth over the cord until the wires are completely exposed." He looked over at me, then grabbed the vase of roses. "I'm a genius! I'll simply knock the vase over and the water will really cinch it." He smiled smugly.

"When they find you, they'll conclude it was an accident. A faulty cord, you received a shock, the flowers fell over and the water spilled. Perfect."

I could no longer keep my eyes open and my brain quit working. I could feel him pull me out of my chair and I folded up like a piece of Kleenex. My eyes were closed and I had no desire to struggle. One little part of my brain seemed to still be alive, but it had no will; it merely recorded, in dim letters.

It seemed that Richard was in the room and he was shouting. Roy screeched threats and someone stumbled over my body. Then mercifully, there was only black velvet.

Many hours later, when the drug had worn off and I was safely propped up on pillows in my bed, Richard sat facing me. Dickie was cuddled beside me.

"Where is Roy now?" I asked, tense as horrible memories came back to me.

"In custody," Richard said sadly.

"Two police cars came!" Dickie shrilled.

"Now, Dickie, you promised you'd keep your voice down," Richard said.

"Two!" Dickie whispered hoarsely and held up two fingers. "And they took Mr. Decker and he had on handcuffs!"

"Let me tell her about it, son."

"Oh, Richard," I said, "he was really going to kill me!"

"I know, my dearest." He leaned forward and took my hand, kissing my fingertips.

"But dad saved you!" Dickie's voice was triumphant.

I had to laugh at Richard's exasperated look, and at how happy I felt. I was safe, I was in love and I was loved!

But there were still so many unanswered questions.

"Did you know Roy—" I looked at Dickie and compressed my lips. Richard let go of my hand and turned to Dickie.

"Son, I just remembered—Louise is probably hungry. You go downstairs and tell Esther that Louise needs a little snack."

"Okay!" he shouted, leaped off the bed and ran out of the room. We both laughed as we heard him thumping down the stairs.

Richard spoke quickly. "Yes, I know what you were going to say. Roy confessed he had killed Vera."

"How did you find out?"

"When I got back from Bakersfield, I came directly to the office, and got there just in time to stop him from putting in the plug that would have killed you. When he saw me come in the door, he came apart like a jig-jaw puzzle. He began to holler at the top of his voice how much he hated me, and how he had planned to turn everybody against me and then he could be pastor. He even hit me, a pretty good wallop on the jaw." He turned his face so I could see the bruise.

"Harry was working just outside in the roses, heard the fight and came running." He shook his head as he recalled the scene. "He held Roy down while I called the police. He never quit yelling and swearing until the police finally took him away."

I was stunned. It was unbelievable.

"But how can Christians act like that?" I finally asked.

"That's what I've been thinking ever since it happened. I

guess all of us, if we aren't allowing the Spirit of God to lead us, are capable of anything."

He kneeled beside my bed and put his arms around me. He kissed me tenderly, but with restraint. He held me tightly for a moment, then rose and sat back down in the chair.

"Thank the Lord for First John 1:9, that 'if we confess our sins, He is faithful and just to forgive us.' But I don't believe a person can continue in sin for as long as Roy has and be a Christian." Richard touched his jaw carefully. He sighed wearily.

"But I'm not to judge, and I don't have the answer, Louise. I've always had reservations about him. But, he said he was a Christian, and he certainly knew the language." He shook his head sadly.

"We need to pray for him. I'm sure he's suffering from some form of paranoia."

After Roy was arrested, he told the police about Harry, the storeroom and his roommate.

Roy's roommate, Leo, worked the "flea markets" almost every weekend. He needed a truck to carry all the things he "bought" and sold and a place to store them during the week. Roy had introduced him to Harry, who was glad to make a little extra money with his camper.

The day the police came to question Harry, all of us except Dickie were in the kitchen.

"I figured they was something a little crooked about it," Harry admitted, "but as long as I wasn't doin' nothin' wrong, I was glad to make the money." He looked sheepishly at Esther who had begun to cry.

"But, honey," he said to Esther, "I knew you wouldn't stand for nothin' that wasn't on the up-and-up, so I never told you. I was tryin' to save a little money for us a trip back home."

"What part did Decker have in it?" one of the detectives asked.

"Mr. Decker didn't do nothin' that I know of," Harry said. "I only worked with Leo. He'd call me and I'd pick him up and take him to some house or other, and he'd go around back and turn on the lights. I wondered if he had keys, but I never asked no questions. I'd help move the stuff out and then we'd store it at the church until he wanted it."

"He told me the first time we went to pick up stuff that he had bought it off some folks that was getting a divorce. I believed him." He looked up at the detective and then down. "Least, I kept tellin' myself I did." He looked up at Esther.

"I got twenty dollars every time I took my truck on a job."

Later we learned that Roy received half of everything Leo got for giving him tips on who in the church and school were on vacation or gone for a weekend.

The police didn't arrest Harry that day, but told him not to leave Los Angeles. Harry told us he had saved almost $500.

"But it'll probably cost me every penny and more to pay a lawyer to keep me out of jail."

"Harry, what I want to know is, who knocked me out on the playground that night?" I asked. "It wasn't you, was it?"

"No, ma'am. It was Mr. Decker. He had come over to see Leo that night at the school. He never had taken any part in it before, and he saw you sneakin' around. But, believe me, Louise, I didn't know nothin' about it at the time. I found you stretched out that night and brought you in, just like I said." He snorted. "Mr. Decker bragged about hitting you, that day in the office, after he went haywire."

Poor Esther cried that day until she was almost sick, but at last she wiped her eyes, stiffened her spine and put her arm through Harry's.

"I'm standin' by my man," she declared.

Shortly after Richard gave me the engagement ring, Vanessa left the church. She had her letter sent to a new, modern church out in the valley. I wasn't sorry to see her go. The last time I saw her, she was talking to Richard in his office, but he had left the door wide open.

"Well, Richard," she had said tartly, "I hope you'll be happy with such a young girl." I was sorting the mail. I could hear every word, and she knew it.

"To think of the years I've wasted in this stupid little church, waiting for you." She swept out with her nose tipped up, without looking my way.

Instead of hurting the church, the publicity seemed to put new life into it. Many new faces were in the congregation each

Sunday. I'm sure some came out of curiosity to see the man whose wife was murdered, or to look at the heroic preacher who saved his secretary.

But they keep coming back, and a few have walked down the aisle to give their hearts to Jesus Christ.

Richard and I have set the wedding date. April 1—exactly one year from the day I landed at International Airport in Los Angeles.